MAUSUMBE ROAD

Subia J. Ali

IBEX READS
California

IBEX READS

This is a work of fiction. Names, characters, places, and incidents either are the product of the author's imagination or are used fictitiously. Any resemblance to actual persons, living or dead, events, or locales is entirely coincidental.

Library of Congress in Cataloging-in-Publication Data
Name: Subia J. Ali, author
Title: Mausumbe Road / Subia J. Ali
Description: First Edition. | California: IBEX READS, 2023

Identifiers: LCCN 2023902329 ISBN 979-8-9877454-0-3
Subjects: GSAFD Suspense fiction.
General fiction. Pakistani American. Suspense thriller fiction.

ISBN 979-8-9877454-0-3 (paperback)

Printed in the United States of America
10 9 8 7 6 5 4 3 2 1

For S. N. H

Table of Contents

MAUSUMBE ROAD

Subia J. Ali

One

They were weightless in my hands, but dangling from my fleshy little earlobes I could feel their heaviness. Especially when I ran down the carpeted stairs, collecting static electricity to give Omar a shock. They would bounce and swing with my gait and in my 10-year-old mind they gave off spears of shimmery light like the blinding glare of a superhero's shield. I wore them that proudly too.

All winter break from school, I'd wake up, brush my teeth, and rush to my bedside drawer and carefully take them out of Baba's cufflinks box. I'd pretend the box was a treasure chest with rusted hinges barely holding it together and ignore the Ralph Lauren emblem printed on it. In it they would lie, beautiful yet lifeless, until they were held up against my ear. "They're so sparr-rkkkly," my heart whispered every time, and into my pierced lobes I inserted them securely. With all my teeth visible, I smiled deeply, then tamed it to an appropriately coy smirk, the way Mom had instructed each time she posed me for pictures.

Wearing them made me feel instantly pretty, the way I imagined makeup made older girls feel. I'd turn my head to every possible angle, getting the sunlight streaming through the slats in my bedroom blinds to hit them so they would illuminate the copper hues in my chubby cheeks, which I inherited from Mom's side of the family. According to Mom, the undesirable *badami* color of my skin came from Baba's side—specifically his mother, my dadi. But Dadi Jaan also gave me my favorite accessory, her heirloom earrings that fed my lifelong passion for jewelry, so I figured we were even.

It was an added bonus that her gift to me was gold earrings which meant two pieces of jewelry, unlike the ring and bangle that my cousins, Urooj and Samreen, in Pakistan were given. To rub it in, I wrote a letter to Urooj with a drawing on the back of two disproportionately large earrings with turquoise stones attached to a tiny brown circle representing my face. This was mailed across the world for the simple purpose of making my cousins jealous of me being Dadi Jaan's favorite.

That year my Dadi Jaan's gold earrings made returning to school after the holidays more bearable. I, for once, had something to show off to my friends as a Christmas present, even though I didn't celebrate the holiday. Every year prior, my friends bragged about what they got from Santa and I couldn't help secretly rolling my eyes.

'Santa . . . right?' I'd learned the internal eyeroll was imperative to the preservation of my friendships after my kindergarten outburst had Mrs. Glover steaming and my parents shamed by a call from her about "respecting other people's religious and cultural beliefs" and "your family should understand that most of all." I don't remember how my parents handled that call but do recall the sit-down they had with me.

Technically, it wasn't a sit-down like the ones my parents and I watched a dozen times on countless family sitcoms. For one,

Mom was standing, facing the open kitchen cabinet with a glass pitcher for company. A plastic lime-green pitcher for everyday use, and neat rows of drinking cups stood nearby—the ajar cabinet door an almost debilitating pet peeve of hers. But with pieces of uncooked *shami kebab* sticking to her fingers, she was helpless.

Baba stood in his usual stance, tall, both hands on his hips countering the weight of his small, protruding belly. His head tilting first right then left, bird-like, then finally looking up at the one blown-out bulb of the recess lighting in the kitchen ceiling. For a moment I thought he would forget all about reprimanding me and I could continue elaborating on the dainty necklaces, and drawing a ring on every finger of the princesses in my coloring book, but the crime of telling Kristen that 'Santa's not even real' warranted parental intervention.

Poor Kristen, how my heart aches even now thinking of how quickly her blue eyes teared up at my declaration. Aidan, Tiffany A., and the kid with the constant runny nose all uniformly erected their heads meerkat-like and looked into the blacks of my eyes. A moment later, I was engrossed with tracing the letter S for Santa page in my kindergarten workbook which I chose to color a shade of fuchsia and Santa's skin, beard, and melted snow puddle, a pee yellow. Later that evening at home with the subtle fragrance of basmati rice filling the house, I'd draw dangly earrings on Santa a shade of yellow, the closest color to gold I had.

"Look here, Hena, you don't need to say to anyone that Santa is not real. You know it's not a good thing to say, right?" Baba asked wearily.

"I think so." I spoke.

"Mushtiaq, she don't know she is not supposed to say that to the children."

Baba shook his head in agreement but before he could better explain things to me, Mom interrupted. "Listen. They think Santa is bringing them presents so why do you have to tell them he is not real? Who cares if he's real or fake? Just mind your work in class." she ordered in one breath and continued slapping the *shamis* into shape between her palms.

Baba pulled out the stool tucked under the kitchen island and leaned in close to me so Mom couldn't hear. "Everybody believes something different. I know you know this. Your friend Kristen and other classmates believe Santa is bringing them presents for their holiday . . ."

"But Baba, Santa isn't bringing Kristen the Gabby's Garden Growing Kit, her parents are."

"I know, Hena, but her parents don't want her to know that. All the children, they believe in Santa so next time try not to say anything about it. Tomorrow, tell Kristen you are sorry as well. ok?"

"Ok, Baba."

"And tell your Mrs. Glover you are sorry too. I will give you the Christmas candy to give to her tomorrow morning." Mom added as she let out an exhausted sigh and slammed the cabinet door closed with her elbow.

I fully intended to contest that the box of assorted Christmas chocolates was a gift handed directly to me by Mr. and Mrs. Murphy from next door and therefore they were mine to eat even though it was followed by a cheery, "Merry Christmas to you and your family." Though noting Mom's stern tone and Baba's nod to me to do as Mom instructed, I was left helpless and candy-less.

The sound of turning pages of Omar's textbook coming from the living room halted as soon as my chat with Mom and Baba was over. Knowing Omar would be able to explain things to my five-year-old brain in five-year-old terms gave me some solace. He broke it down to me with an anarchist teenager's perspective.

His skinny arms flailing, he spoke wildly about Santa. I heard *you're right* which brought a smile to my plump face. He continued with Mrs. Glover being racist for telling Baba that our family should know better and that a kindergartner should not have to keep the identity of the fat guy in the chimney a secret for the sake of the other kids. "Mom and Baba's apologetics are sickening and that Glover is still the same bitch she was when I was in her class." At the time I understood only bits and pieces of what he said but my soul agreed with every word. It was opposite of anything Baba and Mom were saying, which was pretty much, 'apologize and give your teacher your Christmas candy as penance.'

TALKS LIKE THESE WITH MY parents and the re-talks later with Omar helped me see that Mom and Baba weren't always right. Most of all, I was comforted by a big brother who could help me navigate through life with our immigrant parents. Rare if ever were reprimands, scoldings, or sit-downs with Omar. However opposite his views were to theirs, he never voiced them—even though I often wished he did, if only to show them how similar I was to their favored child. He rarely opposed them, as if whatever he had to say would have fallen on deaf ears or lost in some Urdu-English translation.

Throughout high school and college Omar was on various debate teams, Indo-Pak clubs and the Muslim Student Association.

He was passionate about equality and freedom of speech but at home he listened more and spoke less. Mom didn't worry about him getting into trouble or upsetting any racial or religious balances. I was the chubby nuisance, the child they had too late in their lives, a child they could provide far better for financially but didn't have the energy to deal with.

Dadi Jaan was the only one who cared to illustrate my importance in the family. "Allah put so much *rizq* in your family's life through you. Just within a few days of your birth, your baba was able to finally buy the company he'd been working at for years and by the time you started teething, he was planning on how to add another business. Such an auspicious child you were." On our visits to Pakistan, I'd had her tell me that story dozens of times. She'd add new details each time, lending magic to my existence. Especially, when I was younger, I was often left out of joining the rest of the family on their trips to Mari or Lahore because I got carsick. Then, there were the motorcycle rides around the neighborhood with Omar and our *chacha* that I was excluded from because I was too little. In reality, I would be in the way when they checked out the pretty four sisters that lived down the street. The sisters hung out on their rooftop in the evenings flirtatiously giggling and tossing their hair around until one by one they got married.

Baba and Mom moved to Chicago from Pakistan right after they got married, Mom a mere 20 and Baba, 27. They finally settled in Orange County, the most Pakistani-saturated community in Southern California. They had been in the States for ages but still hadn't lost their Pakistani-ness. Mom's cultural identity only sharpened as she got older. My closest friend next to Kristen was Marium, whose Pakistani parents didn't resist the assimilation of the American part of their, or their children's, identities.

Whenever Baba let me have an extra cookie with a wink of his eye, Mom had to pipe up, saying he was spoiling me. "It's a biscuit, dear, no harm,"

"Cookie, Baba," Omar would nonchalantly correct without embarrassing him.

"Cookie, biscuit, whatever it makes for chubby, chubby girls." Mom couldn't resist saying.

It didn't take long for me to understand that chubby didn't mean cute after the toddler age and I started to have my cookies in secret. Mostly I savored them during recess or lunch at school with unabashed cookie eaters. Slowly Mom started to monitor other things I ate. She poured me the smallest portions of whatever *salan* was being served over scant steaming white rice, the smallest for "the smallest and cutest member of the family," she'd coo, while handing me what felt like rations.

She'd altogether stopped serving food at the table where I could help myself to seconds. Baba, Omar, and I standing in a buffet line at the stove with Mom waiting until my turn to dish out what she felt was a reasonable amount. As soon as I'd figured out what she was doing, I'd up the ante and ask to serve myself like a *big* girl. When she caught on, she insisted I was going to burn my wrist on the hot pots because I was too little to reach. I'd pull up a step stool and she'd use a taller pot. I'd ask Baba or Omar to give me more and she'd volunteer herself to get it for me instead. I'd ask Mom to bring me large fries with my burger and she'd come home with a disappointed frown, "Oh no, they forgot to give me the fries." This from a woman who once drove 30 minutes back to Kickin' Wings for the free extra sauce in the tiny plastic container they neglected to give her. I was onto her and she was onto me.

I wasn't aware of it then but her vigilance over everything I ate dented our relationship and my psyche forever. Whenever Mom shamed me about not fitting into a pair of jeans or sighed letting out the seams to the *shalwar kameez* she wanted me to wear to the mosque during Ramadan events, I'd go to bed arguing with her in my mind. Almost always I had a recurrent dream that I was losing all of my teeth and then walking off the Wilshire building in LA that Baba took Omar and I to, once. The jarring nightmare had me jump out of bed and brush my teeth so aggressively I'd spit pink into the bathroom sink.

Omar would always alert me to Mom's prized pearl white Lexus pulling up in the driveway. His lanky figure walking smoothly past the kitchen with a head tilt in the direction of the front door meant I needed to stop binging on whatever prepack-aged goods were in the pantry and wipe away any evidence from my mouth. I'd mastered the art of using my hand as a plate with my fleshy fingers tightly pressed against each other, not allowing any crumbs to fall through the gaps.

Though Baba never said anything to me about eating or over-eating, I felt my self-respect obliterate whenever he caught sight of my feet from under the pantry door and gave me a disapproving nod. The no-shoes-indoors policy was perfect for stealth attacks on scavenging pantry rats and other behaviors requiring secrecy. It didn't matter that he would take the offending food on two plates to his office, which he adoringly called The Tea Parlor and ask me to join him for a cup of chai. All of my childhood friends into adulthood mimicked Baba's tea parlor with their pinky up every time we held a vessel with a handle.

"So nice of you to come, please, please take a seat. Tell me how are things, Miss Hena." He would encourage the role-play while gracefully pouring his leftover chai into my pink toy teacup and later into my favorite Cookie Monster mug with the words, *for cookies* emblazoned on its shiny porcelain surface. On the plates, sweet or savory snacks. Of the salty variety, Baba's and my favorite crisp Pringles, cascaded out at will. Whether there were more for him and less for me was totally disregarded, but of course there was always more for the guest.

"Things are good . . ." I would answer shyly. Once the shame of being caught secretly snacking dissipated, I'd warm up with, "I guess things are good . . . except Blake was so rude to Abbey yesterday and then we took his basketball and hid it in the girl's bathroom . . ."

When my rambling grew fast with my munching, he would slow things down, "Pardon me, dear, but you must speak slower. I cannot follow your story and also you must speak in a sophisti-cated accent in the tea parlor."

Around the same time, I transitioned to having a favorite mug, I started learning the art of chai making and began coming to the tea parlor on my own, not needing as many cordial invitations, but still taking care to bring two cups of hot chai and two plates for Baba and me to share my cravings on. This happened mostly while Mom was working late, making schedules at the lab. In the tea parlor, Baba caught up on work at his computer and I did homework or used up Baba's printer paper making origami gem shapes. We'd still chat when Baba took breaks to stretch his back in his chair and I would take his cue to pause for a snack. A few dunks of madeleines in our chais, little questions on whether he liked a sketch I'd done, and we'd immerse ourselves back into our own work. Instinctively he and I knew to wash the dishes of our tea meetings before Mom came home, but around my teens, I purposefully left them in plain sight. It wasn't a rebellion against Mom, rather a poke at Baba's complacency.

Two

High school was starting and the chubbiness I sometimes felt I fought hard to keep to spite Mom was literally weighing me down. Sure, I always wanted to be thin like my best friend, Kristen, and other girls I knew at school or saw on TV, even those that Mom pointed out in her weepy Pakistani soaps while she had her cup of chai and sulfur-smelling Nimko snacks but I also wanted to eat without fear, the way I did in the tea parlor. The only other time I felt free to eat without judgment was on our family visits to Pakistan. I went to Pakistan at least every other year from the time I was born until my first year in college when Baba had a falling out with his eldest brother, Kuli. Prior to that, our visits were usually for weddings of cousins, over Dadi Jaan's health scares, and once over an inheritance matter. I anxiously anticipated every visit to Pakistan where I felt perfectly satiated, not just with food but with the kindness and praises I was bathed in by Dadi Jaan. She cooed over my fearless smile and youthful heart-shaped face. Mom felt it was inappropriately welcoming and the chubby face, lacked dimension. But Dadi Jaan celebrated my visits by sending out 12-year-old houseboy, Rehman, to fetch a box of my favorite Pakistani confection: the coconut *barfi*. She insisted on feeding it to me with her own hands even when they grew stiff with arthritis. Being fed by hand as a young adult would have seemed awkward but I welcomed her attention at any age.

Dadi Jaan loved to feed not just me but everyone. Baba's family discussed everything over dinner, seated around a long boardroom-like dinner table with the clear plastic cover protecting the doily table cloth and the mahogany wood peeking through all the layers. *Eat* was one of the few words my dadi knew in English, which she often used as a segue from topic to topic or to end frivolous arguments with the potential to become lifelong grudges.

"Poor man he worked all his life at the shoe store and just dropped dead of a heart attack, but Allah decreed it was his time . . ." Dadi would interject, "Eat, eat!" Or "Sure, he's my brother but why should I visit him if he doesn't have the respect to give my son a congratulations for his graduation?"

"You're right but still . . . now, eat, eat!"

All she had to do was say *eat* and we would move on by swiping savory *masala* across our plates with chunks of meat in between fresh naan morsels and do as she instructed. Mom's disapproval and urge to control us would stay smoldering inside of her, out of respect for the queen mother but she would let it out in whispers to Omar and me whenever she couldn't resist.

Thia Kuli once noticed Mom mouthing an answer to Omar when a family friend at our cousins' somber *nikah* ceremony asked him about his plans for college. Kuli didn't miss his chance to jest, "You and your sister are little ventriloquist dummies on your mom's lap." To which Mom's eyes became thin black slits and she snapped back, "You're one to talk, you need signed consent from your wife, more detailed than this *nikah* to even come to a family event." Needless to say, that sparked further contentions during our visit since Kuli's wife had a reputation for meddling, especially when it came to the family's inheritance, with my dadi's house being the most controversial of assets.

The next few times we visited Pakistan; we didn't even see Thia Kuli but I heard the heated arguments Baba had with him over phone calls. Immediately after, he'd cool off by calling Chacha—Baba's favorite and younger brother, the keeper of Baba's secrets and caretaker of Dadi Jaan, with the help of his pretty young wife, Shena, who sadly joined the family just in time to tend to Dadi Jaan's increasing health issues, which she lamented to Mom sent her into premature aging.

I wanted those arguments about inheritance and selling Dadi Jaan's home to erupt so we could make another trip to Pakistan to sort things out. But by the time I was in high school, I dreaded Baba's shouting matches with Kuli. They only meant Dadi Jaan, my biggest fan, was close to death. Right before my last visit, Omar didn't help my anxiety. "They're both scavengers circling over Dadi Jaan. I'm not going to be a witness to it this time." he fumed. He did stay back that spring, leaving his wedding shopping for traditional wedding wear and jewelry—to be given to the newest member of our family, Ayesha—entirely to Mom and me.

Mom and Baba cautioned me against going to UC Santa Barbara over UC Irvine in the fall. Their reasoning was tied to Obama finishing his last term and the rising tide of Islamophobia across the country. According to them I'd be safer at Irvine in the Muslim-dense community of the OC. While their parental concerns were valid, I knew they just wanted me close to home. Needless to say, I settled for the more pleasing option of UC Irvine.

The disappointment of abandoning the idea of moving away for college and the past two years of a strict diet beckoned me to

Dadi Jaan's embrace and her permission for me to *eat*. Attention from boys and the jealous cattiness of girls at school replaced my cravings and had begun to give me a different kind of satisfaction. Mom insisted that I could afford to be thinner, just in case I gained a little back, to which I rolled my eyes. Yet, I ate certain foods in extreme moderation, doused with the fear of gaining the weight back; a pinch of the coconut *barfi*, more meat without the oily *salan*, less rice and naan, and of course pastas and baked goods I almost entirely forbade myself.

I got a membership to Yoga Soul and Mom came to a class with me on a bring-a-friend-free day. On our way home in the car, she declared yoga couldn't do much for weight loss and encouraged me to join the gym instead. It was pointless telling her I chose to take her to a gentle yoga session on account of her bad knees, and myself preferred the vinyasa flow classes in a heated room where she wouldn't even make it through the warm-ups. But like Omar, I found it futile to explain and risk an argument.

Once, Mom and I ran into Marium and her dad at the Sahara Market to get fresh pita bread. Her dad asked if I could now do a fancy handstand thanks to all the yoga classes I'd been taking. My mom inserted, "They just breathe and stretch in there, nothing for the body." I shot back, "You're cynical about everything, Mom. You don't give anything a chance." That evening Mom gave me the silent treatment over dinner, with Omar and Baba shooting glances at each other, suspecting we must have had another one of our usual quarrels.

What Mom missed in her one yoga class, I found; a moment to breathe at a time when I felt like I was suffocating under the pressures of being a young woman. The hot air that my lungs exhaled while holding on and letting go of each posture demonstrated to me that my body was capable of change and food needn't to have such power over me.

Besides the help of yoga, I escaped my lust for confections with the simple sweetness of getting lost in drawing and sketching on a sleek, glossy tablet that had the same weight and smoothness of a plate of food on my lap. At first, transitioning from a paper sketchpad to the cold of an electronic tablet felt blasphemous but once I worked out the kinks of drawing on a screen, it felt as natural as paper.

Of all the self-help blogs on weight loss I'd scrolled through, there were never suggestions to look for joy in things other than food. But I found joy in sketching beautiful ideas for baubles: lines on paper that started off as scratches turning into intertwining vines, where your eye could follow along a maze of shapes and come to an opening, illuminated by a gem. Seeing a piece of jewelry in my mind and transferring it to a visible idea in a sketch gave me a similar sensation to eating my favorite foods.

Still, that Spring I looked forward to having a food fest with Dadi Jaan in Pakistan. During that visit Mom was tasked with Omar and Ayesha's wedding shopping. Baba was readying and signing inheritance documents that Dadi Jaan insisted be completed while she was still alive. I hugged Dadi Jaan's small body, feeling my fingers gently settle in-between her ribs. I could feel her soul spilling out of her body even though she struggled to live for two more years. She spoke less and moved with a walker. By the time Rehman came back with the usual box of *mithai* for her to feed me, she had often fallen asleep, sitting on a chair on the porch with her head cradled on her arms that rested on her walker. Even if I could have overcome my food fears just for that trip, seeing the sadness well up in Baba's eyes at his mother's condition made everything unsavory.

Baba spent most of his time either reading the newspaper to Dadi Jaan at her bedside, on the account of her weakening eyesight, or sitting on the porch outside her room with chai to discuss the ongoing inheritance issues in the family. Mom busied herself with shopping for Omar's wedding, bullying me into her favorite clothing boutiques and putting off jewelry shopping until Baba was free and could join us. I slumped in the corners of shops and got lost on my phone, texting Kristen and Marium about the miserable time I was having, swatting mosquitos and fanning myself with a flyer for an art exhibition I would never attend. Mom knew my energy was dwindling and began bribing me with pistachio ice cream, then negating it with "let's find you the best outfit to highlight your new tiny waist. You know you're next in line. Everyone's parents will be asking me about you at the wedding." For a moment excitement filled me at being showered with attention but it was replaced with a painful rumbling in my belly and the thought that I couldn't afford to take Mom's bait of ice cream since cream and sugar were not conducive to a tiny waist.

Food poisoning however saved me from being Mom's shopping mule too long during that visit. Instead, I stayed home with Dadi Jaan, resting in her bed on the side closest to the bathroom while she reclined next to me whispering *"As-salaam, as-salaam, as-salaam"* on each prayer bead. Another set of her jade beads caught my eye and I wrapped them around the fevered skin of my wrist and watched its silk tassel gently dangle. Dadi Jaan paused in between her incantations to give me a bobble of her head, impressed by the prayer beads turned-adornment.

After two days of vomiting and diarrhea, I was not only starting to feel better but I was also thinner, the size Mom had suggested I reach. The clinking of chai cups against their saucers and soft murmurs of Baba, Chacha, and Dadi Jaan woke me from my nap. They all sat cross-legged on the bed.

"Good, you're awake." Dadi Jaan spoke softly. Spread out across her bed were about a dozen pieces of jewelry, various earrings, rings, and even her wedding *tikka* and *jhumar*, duller than the other pieces but having the same vintage charm of the earrings she'd given me as a kid. In a neat stack were papers with crescent moon and star stamps. At their glowing sight, I immediately sat up. An informal meeting was taking place where she was laying everything out for her family so nothing was left unresolved after she was gone. Except Thia Kuli was missing, refusing to attend if he was not going to be named the executor of her will.

Tucking my curls neatly behind my ear she started speaking in Urdu to Baba. "She's just like me, you and Parveen don't see it but she is. She loves with her whole heart and has an eye for beautiful things." Her fingertips danced on the prayer beads I wore as she continued. "I wish I could give you more, Mushtiaq. Kuli may be older in age but you've always been the sensible one. I know I won't be in this world long but I have had a blessed life, I'm so grateful for you and this girl you have raised, she lights up my heart. She is your rarest gem." Baba's sobbing stopped her from going on. Her eyes opened wide, she declared, "Stop this crying. Hena, pick whatever you want." I looked to Baba for approval and he nodded in permission.

I picked up her *tikka* and *jhumar*, laid it down, going back and forth between it and some of her dainty rings as she encouraged me to take a more valuable piece, pointing at an all-gold necklace with earrings and a ring to match. But I wanted the pieces I'd seen her wearing in sepia-colored pictures of Mom and Baba's wedding. Its nostalgia lured me. It was meticulously made by hand to which belonged the story of her wedding day where its gold glow lit up her face so much to her liking that she'd worn it to sleep on her wedding night, creating a slight dent in the *jhumar*'s filigree where it pressed against the side of her forehead and pillow. The dent was still visible, she had tried to get it straightened out at her family's favorite jeweler in Saddar, the same jeweler she insisted Mom shop at for Omar's wedding jewelry. No one had the heart to tell her that the jeweler passed away years ago and his shop had permanently closed.

Dadi Jaan validated my choice holding the *tikka* up to my forehead with her shaky hands. "You have good taste. These have a kind of life that the others don't." Later Mom would scold me for making a foolish choice by picking such outdated jewelry. To prove a point, I wore it to Omar's wedding that summer back home. At his unnecessarily elaborate wedding, Mom was inundated with questions about my age, college aspirations, and thoughts on marriage by mothers looking for brides for their sons. Baba detested such questions and archaic marriage talk and had Mom promise not to indulge in them until I was out of college and on a solid career path. But Mom snuck around upselling me as an 'assimilated girl' and 'best of both worlds', mentioning the dozen times I'd been to Pakistan.

My knowledge of true Pakistani culture was limited mostly to what I learned from Dadi Jaan and tedious shopping trips to bazaars in Pakistan with Mom. Other times were during the occasional family trips to the Karachi beaches with my cousins, when our families were on speaking terms or when I was attempting to play cricket with the Pakistani born-and-bred kids in Dadi Jaan's neighborhood. It meant I hardly bled green and white or even spoke the language without messing up masculine and feminine.

Mom's praise, however exaggerated, and her constant mention of my new thinness gave me the ego boost and iron will I needed to resist even the slice of wedding cake staring me down at Omar's wedding from under the overflowing centerpieces.

I remember having to video call Dadi Jaan so she could be a part of the wedding. She squinted just trying to recognize my face and relied on her hearing instead. Chacha and Shenachi had me show them everything from the wedding cake to Ayesha's bridal jewelry, awkwardly close up. Dadi Jaan was in good spirits in spite of having been on bed rest because of unexplained heart palpitations. Her visits to the hospital became more frequent over the next two years, and Baba and I were almost desensitized to hearing about her health scares.

Three

Baba held his head in his hands like it would drop off if not anchored. Omar held Baba's shoulder, attempting to ground him in the same way while Ayesha sat on her hands, her doe eyes stunned at seeing her calm father-in-law in a panic. Omar and I had only witnessed this trepidation in Baba a few times. Once, when Omar broke his collarbone at basketball practice and Coach Jimenez nervously called Baba informing him that Omar had broken his "neck." Then before Baba acquired the second LabQuest.

He was later able to joke, claiming his panic attacks were prophesies. "When you see me like this, something good is going to happen." He was right the last two times but this time, it preceded an ominous event. Before I had the chance to put my bag down and spill the notes on communication theories mixed in with my usual jewelry sketches, Baba stopped and spoke decidedly, "I'm going to get on the next flight to Karachi, pray I make it on time." Like a leaky tap, tears began to drip down my face. Ayesha rubbed my back with one hand and attempted to gather the contents of my bag with the other. Like me, the bag was uncooperative and lifeless, gaping open at the mouth whilst the worn leather skin not giving it the solid structure to allow anything to stay in; a formless matter, having volume but no shape. No soul.

It was inevitable. I knew she was ill but she always pulled through. The reality of Baba going to Pakistan immediately meant she was taking her last breaths. I'd just spoken to her and she was fine except for the short, labored breathing that whooshed in between sentences. Instantly, I regretted not speaking to her longer in my rush to meet Kristen to study for our marketing finals. It gave me some solace that my last conversation with her was at least meaningful. She asked if I had been eating properly since the last time she saw me; I was getting too thin for her comfort. A small smile sprouted on my lips, invisible to her over the phone. She went on with the usual invitations for me to visit soon and her recent favorite topic. "I do want to see you get married in my life-time but your baba insists you have two more years of college but then what? You'll get married and get busy with a family and never discover Karachi. It has layers upon layers: risky adventures, interesting people, all sweeping in on the warm breezes of the Arabian Sea. Hena, your parents wouldn't like me telling you this but living in America you haven't experienced life, you haven't lived. I wish for you to live."

"Dadi Jaan, you make it sound so amazing or maybe it is, but I just haven't had the chance."

"And those beautiful drawings you make, you need to have a jeweler here make it into a real piece of jewelry. I wish I was young and I would take you to them myself. They would still remember me too. You know the money I have spent at those jewelers have paid for their children's weddings." Dadi Jaan laughed until she wheezed, "Come with Omar and Ayesha. I want to meet her too."

"I wish I did that when I was there last but I promise, I'll come after graduation."

She knew how to sell me on another visit since I'd confided that our family picnics to Hawks Bay, Gadani, or the French Beach were a bore and I really wanted to see more of the city, eat the street foods often forbidden to me by Mom. I wanted to live or at least be allowed to come out from under the protective wing of my parents.

The thought that she might not be there by the time I next visited played on my mind but I violently shook it out of my head. The entrancement she'd put me in with her love for her city and the incentive to bring my designs to life had me resolve to one day visit her by myself. It would be just be me and her recklessly eating coconut *barfi* and trying on jewelry—perhaps my own creations. When she breathed a gentle exhale over the phone, I could've sworn I felt it like a breeze across my entire face.

Baba left that day while Mom made phone calls to his secretary, cancelling all of his meetings that week. I packed his clothes and slipped a note into his shoe: *You're going to get through this. Love you, Baba.*

By the time Baba was boarding his flight, I was having my usual reoccurring nightmare. Over the years, it had become more vivid. Falling with crippling fear, my fingers curling in an attempt to grab onto anything but there was nothing . . . just air. I'd see myself falling from every angle; the view from underneath with my hair parting tightly against my scalp and whipping up with my eyes barely visible from the top view. I'd begin to accept the inevitability of dying and recite the *shahada* only to fall into a room of teeth—my teeth. They'd start falling out of my mouth like a waterfall, sometimes choking me. My lips would sink in without my teeth to rest on. I dreamt it for two nights until Baba called to tell us Dadi Jaan had passed away.

He arranged everything for her funeral and gave a substantial donation in her name to an orphanage she gave her *zakat* to during Ramadan where the destitute children were said to be surviving on chai and crackers. When Baba returned home, he seemed depleted, unable to say more than a word to any of us. He didn't take any calls, not from LabQuest or condolences from friends, and to Mom's aggravation declined mourners from visiting. He himself survived that week on madeleines and chai, choosing to sit in the tea parlor alone. Omar handled most of LabQuest's day-to-day with Mom. I'd heard the two whispering about how long he'd be like this and what if he never came out of it. But I knew his pain needed time because I was going through the same though no one but Ayesha noticed.

I too was surviving on chai and mini bags of Lays; at the time, sugar felt inappropriately celebratory. Ayesha brought me up a plate of food and the flowers Kristen had left at the door, since Baba refused to answer it. They sat there all weekend, wilting from the sun without notice. Ayesha set them down on my dresser and the plate on my bed next to me. "It will pass, eat something." she assured. The words tore open my heart and I sobbed for an entire hour into her lap.

I did eventually eat but just enough to survive my sadness. Huge guilt-filled tears fell down my cheeks as I admitted to her, "I don't think I'd miss Mom this much." She nodded without judgment since Mom had started in on Ayesha with not much left to pick on me about.

Baba's silence meant if he spoke, he would surely cry for days. I wanted to tell him I felt the same but I knew he needed time and I just needed him to be ok. When I brought him an especially strong cup of chai, it cajoled him to finally speak. A loud exhale rushed out of my lungs when he shared that he was able to speak with Dadi Jaan just an hour before she died. He explained that her skin was paper thin from dehydration and that her body seemed shrunken down to the size of a child. Dadi Jaan even asked about me and beckoned me to visit. To which Baba admitted to her that I was always my happiest in Pakistan—something I didn't know he was aware of at all. *I was only happy because she was there*, I thought.

SOMEWHERE NEAR THE 26TH HOUR of Ayesha's labor, I donned my cap and gown and marched my way to my seat in the amphitheater. I looked around and spotted Marium coifing her hair that sat in a curled heap on her shoulder. Kristen was taking a selfie she would later tag *FlorencehereIcome*. Baba said he cheered for me as loud as he could but later realized it wasn't even me. Omar and Mom sent congratulations texts and pictures of baby Zain's scrunched up face next to Ayesha's thoroughly exhausted one. I promised Marium, I'd make it to our friend Alexa's all-night grad party in the Palisades after a short visit to see the baby.

"How many people will be at this party and how come I've never met this, Alexa?" Mom inquired while a lactation consultant spoke softly to a sleepy Ayesha.

"I didn't know you had to meet all of my friends, Mom. Anyway, it's just a bunch of girls celebrating, no big deal." I calmed her inquiries.

Omar interrupted. "Mom, should we hyphenate the name?"

"Baba? All of my friends are waiting for me."

Omar rolled his eyes and pulled Baba's attention to the birth certificate.

"Ok, go. Be safe and stay away from that Marium . . . would be better off in Europe with Kristen this summer." he murmured.

Being able to go to Florence with Kristen was an impossibility if I wanted to be promoted to Medical Marketing Specialist from Medical Marketing Associate with no difference in pay. There was that extra week of vacation that was useless since I couldn't go to Florence anyway. Still, Baba used the word groomed a lot to get me into the position with LabQuest's affiliate Medisure, a prosthetic design and manufacturing company for which I was *groomed for the job* by no other than the leading Medical Laboratory Equipment Provider in Southern California and avid dunker of cookies into chai, my Baba. He was disappointed when I refused to take a similar position at either of the LabQuests. His dream of having Omar run one had manifested, leaving Mom and himself to manage the other.

I was good at my job and what I lacked in knowledge I charmed my way through but I could be replaced in a matter of a few scrolls on any employment site. I should've been grateful for the comfy job but it didn't feel right knowing that Kristen struggled to land a decent job while, thanks to Baba, I was practically handed one. Baba did get her an interview with LabQuest's hiring manager after I badgered him. Kristen aced the interview, as I expected her to, and they made her an offer—an offer she graciously declined because the start date would make her have to cut her Italian vacay short.

Baba sniffed, "Of course, she can afford to turn down an opportunity like this. She will find another and another" and rubbed his index finger across his chai-colored skin.

The disappointment of not exploring the alleyways of Florence with Kristen or hooking up with the Giannis there or eating gelato with tiny spoons to keep my portion sizes in check was eased because I wanted to explore more of Ameer and he wanted to explore plans for our future.

He wasn't exactly a contrast from the other guys I'd dated. In the beginning, our relationship was steamy, neither he nor I held back any feelings or needs we had. He was particularly clear that he fully intended to marry me. I usually smiled wholeheartedly at the romantic idea, but it was just that—an idea that I tried to avoid indulging in.

I did open up to him more than any other guy. On our first overnight trip together, which Mom and Baba had to be told was a girl's trip to Joshua Tree, Ameer and I sat snuggled against each other in a blanket, our feet dangling from the back of his Jeep's trunk, gazing at the night sky freckled with stars. That night, I told him about Dadi Jaan's impression on my life, which led me to show him the contents of a folder called Nisa on my tablet. My renderings of rustic crystal earrings, domelike rings, and layers of delicate chains dangling dainty pendants made him say, "I had no idea. When you first told me you had an obsession with jewelry, I thought, don't all girls? But this is more . . . like you have an obvious talent."

"But you've seen me drawing and doodling on your hands, remember the one you said would make an awesome tattoo?"

"Yeah, I remember it took days to come off. It looks like you have an archive here though." He pointed at a folder of sketches dated seven years back.

"That's nothing, I have stuff in here from kindergarten. I literally scanned and stored every idea I've ever had on this tablet. It was an emotional cleaning-house type of thing after my dadi passed away."

"Why'd you ever go into marketing?"

"I've asked myself that question so many times. I guess, I just wanted a somewhat stable career. Something my parents would be pleased with."

"And what do you plan to do with all of this?"

"Nothing, I guess. They're my version of an adult coloring book. It's the only thing I love to do."

I could have told him that I was always pining to bring my ideas from the lifeless screen of my tablet to actual pieces, and that lately I envisioned creating an entire line of jewelry somehow connected to Pakistan. In that moment, I wanted to thumb through my phone and show him an article I had saved almost a year ago and had been rereading practically every month. It was on the jewelry and rug-making artisans that resided in the small villages in Pakistan's Balochistan province. The article was in the same Global Magazine that sat in the lobby of his family's realty group because it paid homage to their homeland. Instead, I reluctantly closed all the files on my tablet. My finger hovered over a folder with dozens of logos I had designed with the name Nisa—after Dadi Jaan—a proud name meaning woman.

Baba met Ameer at an Eid festival where his parents sat in a cramped booth, promoting their real estate agency. They were sandwiched between the Islamic Financing and Halal KFC vendors where hungry customers kept knocking Ameer's realty banner half down.

Ameer handed Baba a fridge magnet in the shape of a house and fearlessly introduced himself. "*Salaam alaikum,* I'm Ameer. It's nice to finally meet you, Mr. Shah." Baba was taken aback at the lack of explanation Ameer gave him on how he and I were acquainted. I stood in between them, searching for some lie to quell the awkwardness.

Mom had been planning for me to meet a suitable Pakistani boy since she saw me skateboarding with the neighbor's grungy son, Tyler, when I was 16 and lectured me on how I was not to be seen with a boy or even think of dating. This was starkly different from Ameer's liberal Pakistani parents who'd invited me to join them on their family getaway to Mexico.

Baba had a few passing words with me about my intentions with Ameer, to which I insisted we were just friends. Mom was furious when I was honest about going to dinner, on a hike, or to the Lord Huron concert with him. She'd fought me on it until she'd heard his and his family's praises from Ayesha's parents.

Omar was silent when the subject came up, knowing I was at a crossroads with Ameer who was pressing me to know where our relationship was heading; suggesting marriage was the inevitable next step. I had hungered for Omar's opinion for months, something I'd always relied on, but he was busy with his own life, wife, child, and running LabQuest, I told myself. But it felt like he was intentionally disconnecting from me, even judging me from a neutral distance for not growing up.

I BLEW OFF THE FINAL meeting at a Medisure trade show in San Francisco to catch a flight back early so I could make it to baby Zain's first birthday party the next afternoon at Omar and Ayesha's place in their newly landscaped backyard. The instant I entered the front door, laughter and clinking of dishes confused me. Ameer's familiar chuckle sent bolts of anxiety through me.

I held onto my own hands as if to lead me reluctantly towards his voice.

"You're home early!" Mom squealed and instantly started to unroll my sleeves and straighten my shirt out. "They're here, just be pleasant." She excitedly spoke into my ear as she ushered me into the dining room. Polite *salaams* were exchanged as beads of nervous sweat streamed from my armpits.

"What a surprise. We were just talking about you." Ameer's dad winked and they all laughed but I didn't get the joke.

"*Mashallah*, there's that beautiful glowing girl." Ameer's mother complimented.

"Since, you were too shy to approach us about it, Ameer decided to call us like a gentleman and arranged this get together."

"Shy about what . . . wha . . .?"

"About getting married, what else?" Baba added.

Once the shock settled, I wondered if the rage in my eyes was visible to Ameer but he smirked, "Surprise!" his hands mimicking an explosion.

Four

"**A** prince among men . . . haha!" Like a ringtone, Baba said every time he heard me talking to Ameer or simply heard the name Ameer. Not that the "prince" had done anything princely to impress Baba but once Baba picked a word or phrase, he used it until he wore it out. Mom only encouraged Baba to continue by glorifying how amazing Ameer and his family were. She was thrilled at finding a frugal wedding-shopping buddy in Ameer's mom. To Mom's surprise, I'd entirely declined a trip to Pakistan for wedding paraphernalia, insisting we could order everything online.

"You used to love visiting, what happened?" she said.

I wanted to tell her that I never *loved* Pakistan, I only loved Dadi Jaan and the way she made me feel—strangely a part of an otherwise foreign country. Instead of answering, I squinted my eyes at her ignorant question. It took her a moment to remember that Dadi Jaan was gone.

With the wedding two months away, I was still in a passive protest, not taking part in wedding preps and insisting "I wasn't consulted when you showed up to propose to . . . uh, my parents, so you can plan all this yourself."

Ameer would chuckle and pull me into his arms. I'd try to reluctantly break away but I would eventually surrender. In that respect, I could agree he was a prince, easily deeming a thing be done and having everyone accept it, a power I never had. Mom began calling Ameer "prince" insisting she was merely translating his name into English. He'd earned that adoring nickname when he spent an afternoon helping her bring down and sort through boxes of party décor from Omar and Ayesha's henna party that she couldn't reach without a ladder.

"Just say yes or no about the cake . . . it's your area." Mom could still fat shame a slender me whenever an opportunity arose. "Tell her to do some decision making instead of leaving it up to your mom and me."

"Hena, just pick."

"I told you, I don't care and it's not my area, Mom. Nudge me when the tailor is ready for fittings and make sure he adds the red beading, please."

"Again, with your wedding dress! Matching that old-fashioned *tikka* and *jhumar* has delayed the tailor even more and the whole thing has cost more than it's worth. Enough with the dress, decide on the cake." The tip of her nose motioned for Ameer to help her out again.

"Ami Parveen, you've done a great job arranging everything so well so far. I know you can pick the cake and have it perfect too. Plus, Hena prefers *mithai* over cake."

"But what about the outdated jewelry, she won't stop obsessing over it and the dress . . ."

Ameer, bored with the conversation, interrupted with a wave of his hand in her direction. "She's going to wear her dadi's jewelry and wear what she wants. That's her contribution to the wedding and I'm fine with it," he said.

Mom conceded with a cold silence. Witnessing Ameer tactfully stand up for me in a house of complacency should have made me his disciple forever. Except his say-so was affecting me in ways I thought I'd left behind ages ago along with my weight.

Often turning to the escape of drawing, I drifted off in meetings at work, later finding doodles of patterns on the backs of unfinalized hearing aid brochures and even once on a final rendering of a hard dental palate to be presented to the whole team. Stress eating had seeped back into my life with binging followed by instant regret. To appease the guilt, it was followed by a run or hot yoga.

Marium rolled her eyes and Omar scoffed at my mention of being stressed at an impromptu yoga session led by me in our dining room to relieve Omar's back pain, and teach Ayesha an easy routine that would help her shed some baby weight. They all claimed I wasn't the one planning anything for the wedding and therefore couldn't complain about being stressed.

After a warming yoga session, I let out an unexpected whimper while everyone lay still in *shavasana*. An alarmed Omar asked what was wrong. A river of complaints about how much I was hating my job, not finding purpose, fearing food again, Ameer's remark on my recent binging, flooded out of me. Marium and Ayesha, in feminist solidarity, caught the last thing.

"Wait, did he say something to you about it?"

"No, well, yes . . . Mom was going on about how my wedding dress was made to my exact size and I couldn't afford to eat cheese puffs and expect to fit into it . . . and Ameer added, yeah, hold back on the cookies a little too . . . and he has said a few other odd things." The yoga mat was uncooperative, flopping and folding while I struggled to roll it and contain my tears but they continued to stream, straightening a strand of wavy hair that was pressed against my cheek.

"What the fuck is wrong with him, you're a perfect size. In fact, I think a little too thin," Marium raged.

Ayesha asked in concern, "Is this something new or has he always been like this to you?"

I expected Omar to demand the answer to that question and console me but he said nothing.

"At Vincenzo's last week he asked me to order a salad before a meal, something like, it would make me eat less of the manicotti. It's just little things like that and like an idiot, I ordered the stupid salad too!"

"I don't want to instigate anything but when I brought Zain over last week, I saw your mom showing Ameer old photos of you. I think maybe that has something to do with it," Ayesha stammered.

Omar shook his head in disapproval of Ayesha's confession.

"Don't shake your head at me. It's the truth. I even told her to put the album away before Ameer got there. She told me he won't care now that you're thin and rushed me into the kitchen to make chai for them."

"I'm sorry but your mom is such a bitch to you."

"That's my mom, Marium!" Omar finally spoke.

I shouted, "Yeah, Omar, she's YOUR mom. How can she be my mom and do sabotaging shit like this to me? It's so sick how you defend her."

He shook his head side to side and began tucking the chairs under the dining table. My sadness began to morph into anger. Why couldn't he continue the argument, giving me nothing at a time I needed him to yank me upstairs like when we were kids and tell me I was right about something.

Everyone avoided the tension in the room and began making their exit. Ayesha snuck upstairs to get baby Zain, Omar put

Zain's teether and baby monitor into the diaper bag. Marium was running late for work and rushed out with a quick hug, "I'll call you later."

She must have texted Kristen a minute after my mini-breakdown on her way out of the house, alarming her that the dance routine she practiced for the henna party may be canceled because Ameer was no prince after all. Another minute later, I was assuring a frantic Kristen over the phone that Marium, as usual, was being dramatic. Ameer was just being a typical guy and her choreographed routine would go on and she needn't worry about me either.

"Guys can be jerks but I know he isn't doing it to be cruel. Hena, don't let Marium rile you up. It's going to be ok, just tell Ameer how you feel." I thought about Kristen's level-headed advice. She could talk me off a ledge and Marium could shout, "Just do it, already!" They both had a place in my life. Although, Marium's voice was speaking more clearly to me this time.

Taking care not to wake Zain from Ayesha's arm, I caressed his head and whispered bye to them. Omar avoided eye contact and fidgeted with the car seat. As they drove away, a cold breeze rustled the leaves of the sego palm. It nudged me back inside the house to the kitchen for a cup of chai where I carefully drew a chai-stained cup out of the cupboard and set it on the granite counter without making a sound, as if any noise would set off some emotional alarm inside myself. Other than the faint jingle of the teaspoon dispersing sugar in the chai, the house was silent. I took tiny sips from the cup and stared blankly at the black screen of the TV, hoping to weigh each hurt in a rational way. Was I overreacting to Ameer and did Mom really cross the line this time or was there ever a line she didn't cross? How could I have been so naïve in thinking my food and body image issue would go unnoticed by

Ameer? If I'd confided in him about them earlier, would he have been gentler with me? He wasn't inherently a jerk.

At the uncertainty, I took long hard sips of my chai with Kristen's sincere advice playing in my head. I forced a laugh at Marium's haste in assuming I would cancel the wedding because Ameer had made a few insensitive comments. When grainy, undissolved sugar at the bottom of the cup slid onto my tongue, tears stung the backs of my eyes again as they had in *shavasana*. I arrived at the same feeling I tried to rationalize out of myself: I wasn't happy and was fundamentally unsure if I could be so with Ameer.

Five

I zoned out a lot, often heard the whistling of the tea kettle without it being on the stove whenever Mom exploded in her rage about my decision to call off the wedding. Ameer's texts piled up, his mom's voicemails began with her crying and ended with threats. Kristen came over every evening insisting I shouldn't be alone. Marium filled my family in on the rumors Ameer's cousins were spreading about me. Ayesha hardly came over or called; Omar said Zain's teething had her losing her mind. Besides telling Mom to "Calm down and take her blood pressure medicine" Baba kept his head down and insisted on going into LabQuest for daily meetings, which he'd stopped going to a year back when he began to consider retiring. I went on hikes in the hills after work to avoid being home with Mom.

I hardly ate and nearly rubbed smooth the ridges that started appearing on my fingernails from some vitamin deficiency just thinking about facing Mom when I'd get home from work. When I did brave getting home, I'd run straight up to my room or the bathroom. Whenever Mom demanded I come out and face her, I sat quietly writing the email in my head I would send to Ameer, explaining why I decided to call off our wedding and by default, our relationship. I'd spoken to him on the phone twice, insisting

I couldn't meet in person until he had calmed down, until his texts stopped being typed in all caps. Ameer's cool-tempered disposition had completely melted. I did my best to briefly explain this wasn't his fault but I know he couldn't hear me over his anger. When he'd pause long enough to let me speak with his shallow breathing settling down, I'd instantly wish for him to start up again because I couldn't put into words a justifiable reason for calling us off. Instead, I shot blame aimlessly at everyone else for their overinvolvement in our wedding, his abrupt proposal, me feeling put down by his comments. Everything and nothing. To which he'd shut me up with a simplistic "Why didn't you say anything all this time?"

Omar's text came moments after I texted Ameer that I'd finally meet with him for the sake of closure. I fully expected him to send me a *fuck closure!* back. Omar, however, wanted to meet me at home while Mom was at LabQuest and Baba at the mosque for a funeral prayer of an acquaintance.

He stood shooting suction darts against the window of his old room. A stream of sunlight brightened one side of his face. I hadn't really looked at him in the last year. He didn't look too different from the day he went away to college or even on his wedding day, except with his hair prematurely grayed around the edges of his face; he was another version of Baba.

I expected him to urge me to reconcile with Ameer, like every uncle, aunt, friends of the family, and the two women who went for evening strolls with Mom did.

"You're right for calling it off. You may regret it later but . . . for now . . . it's ok that you did." He spoke in rhythm with the toss of each dart.

He could have stopped talking then. I would have been at peace having him accept my decision, good or bad. He had more to say and I wanted to hear every word. Making his lanky stride towards the window to collect darts, he paused and slapped away at the air to forgo another round. I seated myself squarely on the fold out.

The gaudy damask print upholstery Mom had the sofa covered in didn't look so out of place since she'd added a golden vase and sprinkled other tacky Persian-style trinkets on the dresser. Her aesthetic in home décor was confined to Omar's room and the guest bedroom by order of Baba who found her sense of style objectionable.

After taking a big sip of air through his teeth, he started, "You need to stop blaming Mom for everything; overeating, for Ameer, and everything else that's not gone right in your life."

"When did you stop seeing how cruel she is to me?"

"You have to be blind to not see what she's like but knowing that she's cruel, how has that changed anything for you? Mom and Baba were and have been difficult with me too and you've seen how Mom is with Ayesha"

"It can't compare to how hurtful she's been to me."

"Mom's a different kind of mean to you but believe me I've been on the receiving end of her wrath and Baba's complacency. Anyway, this isn't a competition."

"Ok, so let's say she's as hurtful to me as she is to you . . . big if, but should I be like you and Baba? Complacent? Just tolerate her?"

He threw his arms in the air and started, "Easy answer? Yes. I've learned that having someone to blame doesn't make things easier. It just gives you a distraction. You're always focused on Mom, wasting your time showing everyone how horrible she's being and how unhappy you are." He took a deep breath and tucked his arms under his armpits before adding, "You freaked out and called the wedding off because it's not what you wanted but it took you so long. You'll be stuck in this rut, not having what you want if you keep blaming everyone for it. It's not Ameer, it's not Mom, it's not food . . . it's you. Figure out what you want and don't make excuses for not getting it. Don't keep playing the victim."

The tortured whistling that was building up in my head while Omar spoke stopped the instant he walked out of the room. Silence filled my ears and I knew there wasn't a last word I wanted to get in. Even if I didn't agree with him entirely, I could see how exhausted he was with me and how exhausted I was with myself. I wrapped my arms around my waist as if they would protect me from the blows of truth.

THAT EVENING I SOAKED in the tub. "What makes me happy?" *What a cringey question*, I thought. I didn't expect an answer but it came anyway with the feel of a draft from the bottom of the bathroom door. It made me sink my shoulders deeper into the warm water. The first images that flooded my mind were of being in Pakistan with Dadi Jaan, then of me drawing contently on my tablet. They made me happy. Not food, not my friends, not Ameer.

I shot out of the water. With wet fingers, I began searching my phone for the Global Magazine article I'd been rereading like a favorite movie until its every dialogue was memorized. Under the beads of still water on the phone screen, the words Balochistan, women, and jewelry were magnified. Photos of women dressed in heavily embroidered *shalwar kameezes* and men in bright-white turbans and black mirrored vests posed, showing off their villages' work; a closeup shot of a row of wool rugs in deep reds and rustic handmade coin jewelry next to an illustration of a map of the area. I traced a road with my finger that led from Karachi to Balochistan. It climbed further into the Quetta Mountains near Chaman and led to Ziarat with a marker showing a historical site, Quaid-e-Azam Residency. The article explained it as the final home of Muhammad Ali Jinnah, the founder of Pakistan—a bright-green gabled-roof estate dusted with snow. A yellow arrow pointed to a cursive font next to the body of the article, *Flora and Fauna of Interest* with mention of the largest juniper forests in the world. More engrossing to me were the small villages dotted on the map of the various tribes that nestled themselves in the snowy mountaintops who created the rustic jewelry in the photographs.

At the sight of the snowy region, a chill crept up my spine, making the tiny hairs on my arms rise. The climate and terrain were vastly different from crowded Karachi, the only place I'd ever visited in the country, where monsoon rains and hot humidity were the only temperatures, I'd known on spring or summer vacations. In SoCal, where consistent sunshine gave me permanent flip-flop tan lines on my feet and naturally lightened the ends of my hair, snow was a rarity, seen in the distance on the peaks of the Angeles mountains or experienced on impromptu snowboarding adventures to the peaks of Big Bear Mountain.

My thighs appeared magnified under the water and I instantly pulled them out, reassuring myself that I was still thin. *Pathetic,* I scolded myself and sunk back under the water, which filled the hollows of my collar bones and then flooded my ears. Under the soft swishing of the water, I focused on the nagging voice that told me that a lone female couldn't travel to Balochistan but it was possible to make a lone trip to Karachi, go back to Dadi Jaan's home and, who knows, maybe show my ideas for Nisa to the jewelers there or maybe just sort myself out.

I'd soaked in enough thoughts when my fingers began to prune and the bathwater felt too cool to soothe. *I'm coming* I whispered, as if declaring the intent would solidify my decision. I knew I never stopped aching to be near Dadi Jaan. Though she was long gone, I believed a part of her must still linger in her house and in her city, waiting for me to return to give me some desperately needed guidance. I was certain that all I had to do was be there.

By the time I got out of the bathroom, I'd mentally packed for the trip. The harem beach pants with the leaf print and all of the long tops that even slightly resembled tunics were in— anything that could modestly cover my torso plus some portion of my behind was also in and anything crop-toppish no matter how feminine, was out. Long maxi dresses with even a cap sleeve could do with cardigans in faint fabrics just in case I got any disapproving stares from Chacha and Shenachi at my immodesty.

Buying travel essentials and wrapping up projects at work that were long overdue kept me busy for the next few days. Marium and Kristen planned a farewell lunch at a tapas bar for me. Halfway through, Kristen asked how my parents took the news of my sudden trip and I pretended not to hear her. By the end of our lunch, they both stared at me in pity. Marium let out a dissatisfied sigh, rolled her eyes, and finished off her strawberry mojito.

"I'm telling them tomorrow. I wanted to have everything ready so I couldn't back out."

"But you're leaving in two days, they're going to flip!" Marium stated the obvious and chewed on her straw.

"I'll pray for you to stick to your guns, sweetie." Kristen's thumb wrapped around the strap of her purse that pressed on her freckled shoulder but she managed to mime prayer hands in my direction. Somehow it was easier to be my Pakistani self with Kristen than with Marium. Whenever I showed timidness about telling Baba or Mom about wanting to go away for summer camp, to the homecoming dance, on a girl's trip to Mexico, or even to a work retreat as a full-grown adult, Marium would be there to scoff at my apprehension.

Just like most traditional Asian parents, mine didn't allow me to really grow up. It didn't matter how old I was. I would always need to get my parents' approval or, at the least, validation for practically anything I wanted to do or be. It was just a cultural norm that couldn't be updated no matter what.

Six

I made two strong cups of chai and decided to forgo the palmiers sitting in a neat row in their shiny plastic packaging. My eyes focused on Baba in the tea parlor as I steadied my stride but the cups shook with little tremors on the floral saucers.

"How good of you to come, Miss Hena."

Hearing the *Miss* and not the *Mrs.* filled my heart with a flood of shame and my eyes warmed with tears. Hot chai splashed around in the cups sending creamy brown liquid down its side before pooling in the saucer.

"What's the matter, *beti*?"

I sat the chai and myself down.

"I'm going to Pakistan, Baba. I'm going to fly into Karachi. I know I've disappointed you, Mom, the whole family. Of course, Ameer and even the Murphy's next door. I'm sorry to everyone and I've said it so much it has no meaning anymore and . . . and . . . I'm not running away from the mess I've made either. I'm just so unhappy." I paused at the last word to clear the cry that was overwhelming my voice, "I'm so unhappy and I want to feel like I felt when I was with Dadi Jaan in her house and I know she's not there . . ."

I covered my face with my palms and sobbed into them. I felt Baba's warm hand on my head as he pulled his footstool from under his desk with the other. He sighed with the difficulty it caused him to sit that low. His voice cracked as he spoke. "I know she's not there but the way she made us feel is always there."

He spoke of her and how much he missed her still. It seemed the years didn't make a dent in his grief. It wasn't surprising though, since she made Baba and I feel like we were as essential as sunlight. Baba listened attentively to my plan to visit her gravesite and sleep in her room during my stay and how "I wanted something else."

"What something else?" he rested his index finger across his gray mustache and scanned my face while I spoke fearlessly to him for the first time of my ideas about creating Nisa. His finger slid to his mouth concealing a tremble of his lip at hearing my grand vision for a jewelry brand named after his mother.

He allowed me to speak, only interjecting to ask simple questions and gave either a *hmm* for confirmation or a squint for me to clarify. Two hours later, the tears that started this conversation were visible only in the smeared eyeliner at the edges of my eyes. The tea parlor buzzed with ideas, akin to a marketing meeting about to finalize the launch of an exciting new product. Baba, of course, played the CEO role for most of his life and knew a good idea from a bad one, instantly. I'd told him about the villages in Balochistan that could create the perfect pieces for Nisa, but he suggested I try finding craftsmen in Karachi who were more reliable.

I expected resistance from Baba about the entire trip, but his pointers and the time he gave me to speak meant I'd sealed the deal. His desk was scattered with torn pieces of scratch paper where I'd scribbled quick sketches of rings and a coin pendant while I waited for my laptop to fire up. He gave me business cards of the jeweler friends he wanted me to visit in Karachi and I showed him the contents of the folder on my desktop that I'd renamed *For Nisa,* after Dadi Jaan. It felt like a love letter to be found years after someone's death. A collection of tiny thumbnails of images and notes reflected in Baba's dark eyes. I pitched my lifelong business idea to him over two hours and two humble cups of tepid chai.

I warned Baba that I didn't have the strength to tell Mom about the trip or the stamina to explain the possibility of Nisa to her. She thought of me sketching ideas for it on my tablet was the same as her playing Scrabble on her phone: a fun waste of time. Yet often she consulted me on which piece of jewelry looked best when she got dressed up for special events. "There's no need to tell her you're going there to research a business idea. Just tell her you need a break; this trip really should be for pleasure anyway," said Baba. Of which she felt I deserved none. "I advise you to make the most of it though and not come back without either taking a break or taking a chance. How long do you want to visit for?" A month, I told him.

Happiness is a strange feeling, I thought. At least when you've gone without it for long. You almost don't recognize it when you feel it again. It's subtle, like the effervescent mist of a soda tickling the tip of your nose – only before you drink it and only noticeable with deliberate effort. Just like that, I began to notice it.

I MUST HAVE BEEN SOMEWHERE over the Pacific Ocean when I peered through the window into the parting clouds. I hesitantly took layers of clothing off, layers that I was urged to put on by Mom's concern that I'd be cold on the plane, was instantly freeing. I knew her true agenda was to have me dress modestly to avoid stares from other Pakistani passengers who may or may not know her family through six degrees of separation in a city inhabited by 16 million people. It was highly probable that at least one or two other passengers on my flight would know a member of my family. If not in Karachi, then at least in the OC, which has a Pakistani subculture of its own.

I read over the same line in my book for the tenth time when I decided to give it up all together. I didn't want to read, I wanted to think. I held back the lump in my throat that wanted to swell to a cry, thinking of Baba's generous cash gift for Ameer and I to put down towards our house after the wedding or to take a trip somewhere. He'd transfer it to my savings "with or without the wedding" I knew I would use it somehow for starting Nisa—an homage to him for his faith in me. He added that I could use money from my Pakistani bank account which he opened for me years ago upon Dadi Jaan's request. She insisted on leaving me some inheritance in Pakistan, feeling it would give me more incentive to visit her homeland even after her death. Before we left for the airport, Baba searched through a manilla folder. He handed me a card with the account number with passwords that were typed out. He'd made the extra effort of having his secretary laminate it. I didn't have the heart to tell him I was just going to take a picture of it and didn't physically need it.

Having slept for most of the flight, my body felt stiff and my skin oily—a mark of good health and youthfulness, Dadi Jaan used to suggest when I would aggressively wipe my favorite orange blossom-scented wipes across my forehead in front of her vanity table. I decided to forgo the cleansing ritual that lay in my bag, the same slouchy leather bag I used in college that seemed to never run out of room, its hidden pocket on the bottom like a secret passageway, concealing a tiny case of birth control pills to a thick encyclopedia. The vibration of the landing gear beneath me knocked the key chain that hung from the bag's zipper pull onto my bare toes, its cold metal cooling my anxiousness. I was finally back in the place that cradled my fondest childhood memories.

HUMIDITY IN THE ATMOSPHERE HIT my skin as I made my way out of the terminal and followed a path lined with metal barriers at the busy Jinnah International Airport. Scanning the faces for the familiar ones of Surghum or Chacha simultaneously was difficult.

"Hena bibi! Hena bibi!" A man's voice called and disappeared. At home, hearing my name called out couldn't be mistaken for anyone else, but here, I had to remind myself, it could be the name of a dozen other girls.

"Hena bibi, here!" It called again and the face of an aged Surghum appeared, fighting his way to the front of the barrier and commandeering my suitcase trolley. I should have recognized him but the salt and pepper of the hair on his temples had dispersed evenly throughout his whole head and deep-set wrinkles made his face droop with the weight of his thick skin.

"As-salaam alaikum Hena bibi." His tall body awkwardly bowed a bit in my direction. Before I returned the greeting, he briskly walked past the hugging families and their teary smiles. I tried my best to keep up but he made a sudden left leaving my footing confused.

"You're so fast!"

"Yes, there's still a lot of petrol left in this old body."

"Your chacha couldn't come but he gave me strict directions to bring you straight home in time for breakfast. You must be hungry."

"I ate on the plane."

"But not *unda paratha*." He swayed his head side to side.

The thought of the meal that was so enticing to Surghum sounded heavy after a 20-hour trip. I tried to convince myself that I was now here as an adult, on my own and could refuse or accept anything I pleased. Cultural norms of Pakistani hospitality negated my thought. I knew refusing a labor-intensive *paratha* would be seen as offensive, at least on the first day.

Surghum politely gestured for me to enter the car, the same car he'd driven and maintained for the family for as long as I could remember. I let go of the carry-on I was about to hoist into the trunk when I recalled how upset Surghum gets when someone tries to do his job for him.

He blasted the AC then asked, "Music or no music?"

"Whatever you want."

"Say what you want. This is your holiday, Hena bibi. I spoke to Mushtiaq bhai yesterday on the phone and I assured him whatever you need or wherever you want to go, I am at your service."

"Then, no music," I answered confidently, looking at his reflection on the rearview mirror, to which he nodded "as you wish."

Moments later we began weaving through airport traffic and he started humming a song. Not having to make small talk with Chacha on the way home from the airport was a relief. Witnessing the light of daybreak fill the smoggy Karachi sky, motorcycles rushing to the streets from skinny alleyways, all seen and barely heard over the rushing sound of the car AC and the humming of Surghum's melody was surreal and nostalgic at the same time.

Patches of early morning fog scattered as we entered Mausumbe Road, a name I'd given the street Dadi Jaan's house sat centrally on. The Urdu word for Orange that I'd overused the summer I learned it from Baba. In a childish act of vandalism, I'd reinforced the name of the street by placing a sticker of an orange that I got from the L.A. County Fair on a cement block at the mouth of the street.

The Orange sticker was now worn down but its orange color still visible. Entering the street, my mind was filled with the memory of the day a 10-year-old me wandered down it with the boy named Haider who lived in the house across from Dadi Jaan. He casually gestured for me to cross Mausumbe Road to the tiny convenience store where we were to get my favorite sweet and spicy Pakistani gummy candies. He must have noticed the fear in my timid American eyes when I looked around for a legal street crossing. When he started walking without me, his hand sticking out behind him for me to hold, I had no choice but to brave the junction. Expertly, he led me in-between cars and beeping motorcycles to the store and back towards home again. When we reached the mouth of our street, I peeled the sticker that was tucked in my back pocket and slapped it on the cement block, hoping to impress him. The only other boy whose hand I had held up until then was Omar. Now, I wondered if Haider still lived in the neighborhood. I stared at the house as Surghum and I waited for the green electronic metal gates of our driveway to open.

My carry-on wheels stammered on the tile floors in the hallway. My arrival was not greeted by the voices of Shenachi or my excited little cousin Khalil like when I was a kid. My dadi wasn't there either, looking out of her bedroom window as we rolled into the driveway, the smell of something frying no longer wafting from the kitchen. Dadi's excited voice didn't rile up the house at my arrival and she wasn't there to aggressively nudge the house help to welcome us into the house.

Chacha had messaged me with a *welcome* gif instead, a bouquet of blurry flowers blooming then shrinking. He said he and Shen-achi would be back by the time I got home from the airport and since they weren't home yet I didn't know where to set my things down for the month. I'd made my way down to the TV room at the end of the long hallway when a small girl in a neat but worn maroon head-to-toe *shalwar kameez* appeared. A younger version of Malala Yousafzai, I thought.

"*Salaam alaikum,* Hena bibi, you'll be staying in this room." She shyly pointed to the room Omar and I always had to share on our visits. I looked back on hearing the fading echo of Surghum's shuffling feet walking towards me.

"What's your name?" I asked.

"Silly girl, you haven't even introduced yourself," Surghum reprimanded. "This is Saadia, she is here a few hours a day to help your Shenachi around the house."

"Surghum bhai, you can put Hena bibi's suitcases in this room. I was instructed to have her stay in this room."

Surghum must have noticed the disappointment on my face when I peered into the room with the heavy curtains tightly drawn. "Is everything up to standard, Hena bibi?"

"I'm not . . . I think so." I looked at the TV room wall as if I could see through it to Dadi Jaan's room.

"Hena bibi, remember what I said, all you have to do is say what you want."

"I think I want to stay in Dadi Jaan's room. It's brighter."

"As you wish!" he tried his favorite English phrase, held his palm to the sky and closed his eyes as if to grant my request.

"But your Shenachi specifically instructed for . . ." Saadia's worried little voice followed behind us.

"*Bismillah*," Surghum let out before entering Dadi Jaan's room. I crossed the threshold reciting the same.

It was bright with a musty scent, but it was missing the kind of light that emanates from the energy of the living. When I slumped down on the chaise across the bed Surghum and Saadia took the cue to leave the room. My jet lag was beginning to dig deep into the sockets of my eyes but I didn't want to miss the quiet of this first moment back. Saadia must have placed my kicked-off shoes neatly on the side of the door as she left. Funny how I didn't even remember taking them off. The cooling tiles on the warm soles of my feet slowed my stride around the room even more. I rubbed the sheer curtains between my thumb and index finger the way Dadi Jaan used to when inspecting fabrics I brought home to be sewn into *shalwar kameezes* by her favorite tailor.

I made my way to the window overlooking the front courtyard that was sealed by the fort-like walls that surround almost all well-to-do family homes in this part of the world—a measure for privacy and security. Above that wall, the neighbors' homes across the street stood taller than they did last year when Chacha FaceTimed us to show us his new car. I wondered what additions had been made to this house. Was the upper level being rented out to someone or was it vacant? Could I stay up there and have even more privacy?

I opened the door that led to a raised patio outside the room I used to sit in for hours, dressing and undressing my dolls, and as I got older, I caught up on my summer reading. A backdraft of air flooded the room, the curtains swirled and knocked tiny vials of Dadi Jaan's tea-rose perfume onto the floating vanity. I shielded my eyes against the brilliant sunlight that bounced off the marble floors of the patio. My curls draped back over my shoulders once the air did a round of the room and escaped like a spirit finally released from its lamp.

Baba messaged me before I got the chance. I replied that I was settled into Dadi Jaan's room and having breakfast with his favorite brother and his wife. Chacha and Shenachi, brought home an elaborate breakfast from a popular roadside restaurant in Thutta while visiting their only son, my cousin Khalil. I was grateful for not having to eat an oily *paratha* and fried eggs but cautious of anything else upsetting my American stomach.

After making small talk about my flight and everyone back home, the only noise heard in the (much too large for three people) dining room was the clinking of spoons and quiet chewing of overly salty *nihari*. I observed the graying hair that had finally sprouted on my youngest uncle's head. Shenachi was plumper but her once perfectly round face had hollowed at her cheeks.

Shenachi cleared her throat and Chacha spoke up, "You didn't want to stay in your old room? Shenachi had it all made up for you."

"Thank you, Shenachi, but I really want to be in a well-lit room and honestly . . . I want to stay in my dadi's room."

"Yes, lots of memories there for you." He smiled across the table to his wife who couldn't contest a grandchild missing their grandmother.

"Your baba told me a bit about your business idea. Let me know where you want to go and I'll take you. It'll have to be on the weekends, of course. Our family jeweler should be your first stop."

"I think Surghum will be able to take me around throughout the week. I know weekends can be really busy at the bazaars. Anyway, I'm just collecting ideas for now. No major transactions yet."

I thought for sure he'd insist on taking me but he simply nodded "I understand."

Perhaps my plea to Baba before I left to allow me to try this venture on my own was confided to him over some lengthy phone call or maybe Chacha just didn't want to take time off from work to take me around. Whatever the reason, no family interference or cordiality to worry about was appreciated. Although the thought of being in the bazaars alone for the first time was a bit intimidating.

For a moment I considered reaching out to my cousins, Urooj and Samreen, but with Baba and Chacha not speaking to Thia Kuli, I didn't want to rock the family boat. They too must have heard I was here but wouldn't dare go against their father's wishes to stay excommunicated. Last year they'd commented on a picture I posted of the three of us dressed up for the one Eid we spent in Pakistan with them, after which I messaged them but never got a reply. If I hadn't deleted all my social media apps when crass distant family members started leaving *so sorry to hear* and *hope you're ok* comments on an old engagement post of Ameer and I, reaching out to Urooj and Samreen could have been a possible option. Certainly, they would ask the question everyone, including the cleaning lady at work, asked once she heard the wedding was off.

"So, what's happening with the upstairs area?" I casually asked across the table. Shenachi stopped chewing and Chacha paused, holding a piece of naan on its way to his mouth.

"The thing is that we've been looking for a desirable tenant but it's hard to find trustworthy people. I know your baba wants us to find someone soon."

"No one's been up there since the Attas? Wasn't that two years ago?"

Shenachi and Chacha both shifted in their chairs, sending mouse-like squeaks from the wooden legs.

Shenachi turned to me and spoke precisely, "Yes, it's been a while but with talks of selling the house and with your Thia Kuli constantly at war over it, we couldn't make any quick decisions."

My small talk was hitting some sensitive family sore spots that Baba didn't make me privy to and my simply being here and staking claim to Dadi Jaan's room might have already shaken things up. I wanted them to know I wasn't an informant to Baba and I wasn't here to settle inheritance issues either.

"I only asked because I might want to go upstairs for old times' sake. I remember I used to wake up earlier than anyone else in the house and would get so bored by myself. I couldn't wait until Thia Kuli's family was awake so I could have someone to play with. I would put Chacha's shoes on and stomp up and down the stairs, hoping to wake them."

Chacha chuckled. "I remember that. Urooj would sneak out to play with you but then Samreen would tell on her in that horrible whiney voice that would wake the entire house up."

I imitated Samreen's voice and we both laughed until Shenachi got up and loudly clanked a few dishes together and proceeded to clear the table. It signaled our meal and conversation had to come to a stop.

"Here, I'll help," I said just as Saadia came in and forcibly took my dish from my hands.

"Hena, our new tenant will be moving in two weeks. We know them very well. They are a good family. They have two small children and a cat. Feel free to go up there before they arrive." She nodded in my direction and carried onto the kitchen.

"Chacha, I'm not sure what I did but I didn't mean to offend Shenachi or you."

"Don't worry, Shenachi is just not feeling well . . . but, Hena, also she has done a lot for your dadi and still takes care of this house. She wants to have some say on who and when we get a tenant."

"I totally understand and I won't bring it up again."

Later, the three of us shared chai and more laughs on the porch. Shenachi relaxed a bit and told me to visit Zainab Market for the eclectic jewelry I was fond of but to not buy anything without haggling. She even offered to have her niece go with me but I told her I had a friend here and we planned to scout the markets together.

"That's great! Who is she?" I did my best to add believable details to my fake female friend, Noreen so I wouldn't be stuck with Shenachi's niece who'd faithfully tell her aunt every detail of my day to add to her paranoia. After the sensitive conversation at breakfast, I wanted to keep my distance from unnecessary family drama.

Unpacking what little I had brought, I tried to keep myself awake with the chore and adjust to my new time zone. After taking a hot shower I couldn't help but doze off in Dadi Jaan's bed. Saadia faintly knocked at my door. The thud of dishes being placed on the wooden table in the dining room became audible.

"Lunch time, Hena bibi," she whispered into the door.

"I'm not hungry at all. Tell Shenachi to wake me for dinner instead."

Food was nowhere on my mind. Surrendering to sleep was enticing; that moment between sleep and wakefulness where everything feels perfect. When I inhaled, I took in a sniff of the peach-colored bedsheet under my face. It carried the chemical scent of laundry detergent but just beneath it, there were warm floral notes of Dadi Jaan's tea-rose perfume, a scent that had embedded itself into the fibers of the sheets.

I slept into the next morning and made ample apologies at breakfast and for not waking up for dinner. Though I couldn't remember anyone waking me either. Chacha had to rush off to work and Shenachi was going back to bed.

"Waking up pre-dawn and offering my morning prayer and then reading Quran until it's time to make your chacha his breakfast leaves me loopy if I don't sleep a little after." She spun her head in a few circles as she spoke.

"I can imagine," I said.

Her slippers scratched at the floor when she made her way lazily to her room but stopped short to stammer out, "I can take you shopping later for the casual *shalwar kameezes* your mom suggested you needed." I politely declined, putting it off for another day. She smiled contently, having the day to go about her routine without having to tend to my tasks.

I meandered around the house looking at the family relics in the formal living room that was reserved just for company. The silver *paan-daan* that sat askew on the coffee table had been out of commission since my *dada* died, well before I was born. With no one else in the family to prepare or eat *paan*, it became a mere decoration. Taking out its compartments and putting them back, reminded me of my jewelry boxes at home. *It could make a pretty jewelry box, so vintage,* I thought, snapping a picture of it to add to my collection of ideas for Nisa. Closing my eyes, I felt the engraving on the plaque of the 1920's gramophone. It was something I did dozens of times during my summers in Pakistan when I was in the room as a kid. It filled my boredom while Mom was out shopping with Shenachi, and Baba was having chai in the yard with old friends.

That was the same summer I tried learning to play field hockey and cricket with the neighborhood kids, all of them boys except for the one girl who played remarkably well. After watching them from the sidewalk for two days, Haider from across the street invited me to join. Knowing to speak to me in English, he shouted commands at the others in Urdu. In a rush he introduced himself to me, scrapping the sharp strands of hair away from his sweaty forehead, "I am Haider . . . you're Hira, right?" Before I could correct him, he yelled, "Hira will play left field!" I naturally drew myself nearest the other girl. Almost immediately I missed the ball that rolled past me. "Idiot," she muttered under her breath which scared me to the other side of the street nearest Haider.

I played with them on and off. It all depended on my level of courage or boredom on any given day. Haider often stopped the game to show me how not to hold the cricket bat like a baseball bat which sent out annoyed sighs from the others or gave them an opportunity to make kissing sounds at us. That had me instantly stiffen up—not conducive to playing any game—but Haider didn't look up or shush them even once. He kept his focus pinned on showing me how to hold the bat, catch, and even occasionally bowl, which he referenced was like pitching in baseball.

I learned a lot from Haider that summer. He had this laser focus that I successfully imitated as an adult. Whenever I presented an idea at work that I knew would see opposition from certain colleagues, I'd recall how Haider was not fazed by the other kids in the game. He could tune them out and do what he needed to, so we could all play more efficiently. I played with that group of kids at least twice a week for two consecutive summers, until the summer I started my period. I often blamed it on having to make shopping trips with Mom to get *shalwar kameezes* to wear back home at Pakistani events and both Eid holidays.

A FAMILIAR STIFFNESS HAD BEGUN to develop in my knees. It was the same stiffness I got during finals or extra-long work days sitting at my desk, to which I knew the cure. "I'm going up to the rooftop for yoga for an hour. Would you tell Shenachi that I'm not coming for lunch?"

"Yes, Hena bibi. I can bring the lunch up if you want," Saadia offered. I declined, making my way up the steep staircase, feeling the stiffness in my knees speak louder now. I took deep full breaths as I passed the shiny silver lock hanging on the old wooden doors to the vacant second floor. The last set of stairs to the rooftop were markedly steeper, so I paced my breath. The door to the rooftop was jammed shut and had to be pushed with my entire body strength to open it. Tiny pieces of crumbling wall flaked off and sprinkled on my head. It was obvious Chacha and Shenachi hadn't been up here in years. I couldn't avoid feeling sadness for the neglected parts of this house. When the faded cement floor of the rooftop reflected warm sunlight against my face, a familiar and forceful draft swirled around me. *Another genie freed from its lamp.*

A notable design of homes in Karachi are the flat rooftops fenced with railings for safety. Karachi, like most compact cities, grew up to the sky instead of across the land, with each house having multiple floors. Just like I remembered, this was one of those grand houses with a high rooftop that allowed a view to the Arabian Sea on clear days but this was not that day. It was well past noon, smog and sputtering clouds had filled the skyline.

I unrolled my yoga mat and began with sun salutes and the afternoon call to prayer sounded from various mosques. I resolved to pray after my practice and set my intention for yoga on my personal renewal during my time here. As the sun heated me, postures became more fluid, the nooks and crannies of my body began to yawn awake like the tightly closed doors of this house finally being opened, with each room allowed to breathe.

My eyes searched to find a tertiary spot to help me keep my balance and rested on Haider's house across the street where I recalled once seeing an orb-like image float between the homes. Dadi Jaan believed the orbs were spirits—*jins* traveling from place to place who would upon arrival change back into their original form. I couldn't sleep the night Dadi told me about what I'd witnessed on the rooftop. It would easily scare me now except somehow daylight seemed to dull all fears.

I wondered if Haider would still remember me. I didn't remember seeing him after those two summers, other than a few glimpses of a red backpack on his back when he entered his house. While in tree pose, hoping to somehow ground myself through three floors of house under my feet, I sent a smile to him for his kind attention to me at those awkward cricket games that taught me to quiet the background noise and go for my goal.

At the end of my practice, I sat cross-legged on my mat, letting the sight of my surroundings make their way into my barely parted eyelids. A cat walked carefully across the brick wall down below; a little girl, holding an older bearded man's finger as they strolled through the narrow street, pointed at the eagles sweeping across the sky. The scent of stewing tomatoes came up with the breeze. I began to plan how I'd politely decline lunch and save the calories for when I was really hungry. When I fully opened my eyes, I saw a guy standing under the shade of a gnarly tree in front of Haider's house. His face was partly obscured by the specs of lights and shadows that stenciled through the tree leaves but I could make out that he was looking up at me. I figured he'd move on and I tried to find my way back into the meditative state that was often elusive to me in yoga. After a few moments of struggling with the sharpness of the sun stinging the skin on my arm, I blinked my eyes open again to find him still there.

In my nervousness, I couldn't get my mat into the taut roll I always tried to achieve. Instead, it was uncooperative, flopping around like a fish while I continued to feel his piercing stare on my back. When I felt a frustrated sigh rising from my lungs, I decided I wouldn't be defeated by a lifeless mat or a creepy looky-loo. I turned myself around to wrap my mat correctly and stubbornly stare back at him. Except now, he was on the phone, slowly walking and talking on the sidewalk with a cool smile appearing on his face. I squinted my eyes to see a resemblance to Haider in his face but he could've been anyone from this height.

When his phone call ended, he slipped his phone into the front pocket of his jeans, lit a cigarette, and leaned his body against the gate of his house with me in full view. He brazenly stared at me, not caring about my obvious discomfort. A passing cloud gave way to the sun that reflected bright light off of the whitewashed walls of the homes across the street and stung my eyes until they watered. When my vision cleared, he was replaced by a puff of smoke. As I stood from kneeling, my mat in its sling, a girl with long black hair appeared at his spot, clutching a book tightly under her arm. Her other arm waved hello to me like a windshield wiper set on the fastest setting. Startled to see him disappear, I paused before smiling and waved back. Her excited shouting was lost in the noise of a motorcycle puttering down on the street. I pointed to my ear, signaling I couldn't hear what she was saying. She walked onto the middle of the street and yelled, "I love yoga too!" The veins in her neck strained but her face was relaxed.

"Oh, yeah? That's great." She gave me a thumbs-up and walked back to the sidewalk of her house. Shenachi and the lady next door were chatting in murmurs at the front gate of our house. They both looked up at me smiled and continued their conversation. I pulled my short tee down to ensure it covered all parts of my torso, I was almost certain they were talking about how immodestly I was dressed.

"This is Bushra Auntie, Hena, do you remember her?"

"Sure . . . yes, of course," I lied.

"*Salaam alaikum*, you are enjoying your vacation from Canada?" she shouted in a raspy man-voice.

"Amrika, not Canada, Bushra."

"*Salaam alaikum*, yes, it's a nice break."

"I heard about your situation. Allah knows best. At least, it was only an engagement. It's hard these days for young people," she lamented. Shenachi immediately nudged her, after the entire neighborhood was broadcast my *situation*. Mortified, I moved to the middle of the rooftop where I figured I couldn't be seen from the street and wondered if the disappearing guy had heard our conversation, but more importantly, who was that girl to him?

Seven

I peeked at my phone to see if Ameer had messaged. What if he wanted to meet in-person for some final words like I suggested we do if he could calm down enough? He'd have to wait until I came back, which would upset him further and cast anxiety over my time here. I tried quieting these thoughts by telling myself that he likely knew I wasn't in California anymore. *Running even further away*, he must have thought, and how that must have stung. Him, having to stay and deal, and me, on a vacation across the world.

I kept my messages to everyone back home to a minimum, often choosing auto-replies. Fear of getting caught in a shouting match with Mom over text, fear that if I sent long messages to Omar, he'd think I was open to a conversation on whether going to Pakistan was the conclusion I came to after our last talk or ask some other sensible questions for which I was not prepared to answer. I even kept my texts to Marium and Kristen short. I wanted to be here by myself and with myself and this was impossible to do if I was in constant contact with everyone back home.

"Going for the yoga again, Hena bibi? No lunch today either?" Saadia teased.

"You'll make yourself sick if you keep exercising in this God forsaken heat and not eat proper meals. How you're surviving on that bag of nuts and a few pieces of meat you pick out of your food at dinner, I can't imagine." Shenachi spoke over a hot skillet, wiping her brow with the edge of her scarf.

"I promise, I'll have some of those delicious smelling meatballs you're making."

A few days had passed and I was falling into a far too comfortable routine: waking late, eating a piece of toast to prove to Shenachi that I was eating, sketching a few designs for Nisa, taking long naps at random times of the day, practicing yoga daily on the rooftop with no sight of the handsome guy or the cheery girl, finally, chai on the porch with Chacha after dinner. It didn't sound horrible to rest and repeat but I didn't want the month to pass without a solid attempt at Nisa in the world outside of the house.

I gave into Shenachi's insistence to take me out for the *shalwar kameezes* Mom was obligating her to get me. Just like Mom, she dragged me to clothing and jewelry boutiques, far more Bollywood in style than traditional Pakistani. She ordered a salesman to hand her a rhinestone-studded necklace with fringing silver chains cascading from it and held it up against a busy black *shalwar kameez*. "See how it stands out? Like stars in the night sky."

It was poetic but the furthest thing from the understated, natural jewelry I was looking to create for Nisa. "Yup, it stands out." A dozen pictures were sent to Mom of the two of us at various boutiques; Shenachi holding up lawn outfits against the length of my body for Mom's approval and others of Shenachi leaning in close to me, forcing a smile, with me attempting an equally strained gracious one.

While Surghum was called to pick us up, I managed to buy a long silky tunic and a pair of handmade leather slippers just so Shenachi would get some satisfaction in helping me find a few things I liked. The day shopping with her was as tedious as it was with Mom and I vowed I wouldn't endure anymore of it on this trip.

At dinner over the soft meatballs covered in masala accompanied by fresh naan from the tandoor down the street, Chacha spoke about his new client from New York, a Pakistan-born man who wanted to open a restaurant in Karachi near a popular beachfront shopping center that Chacha had been trying to sell.

"He's a fascinating man. He used to work at his father's rickety chai shop as a chaiwalla back in the 60's. He told me that he recommended his father put out two wooden stools and a small tin table his mother had at home so the occasional *gora* tourists could have a place to sit at an authentic chai café. His father agreed, if his wife could be convinced to let him borrow it." Chacha told the story, pausing to lick his thumb, savoring the creamy masala stuck to it. As he continued, I leaned in over my plate to listen, tearing small holes in my naan with my teeth.

"She gave permission and that's how their business grew. *Mashallah*, the little things that change a person's life forever," Shenachi concluded.

"No. She didn't allow it." Chacha wagged his finger. "But he still took it to the chai stand every day while his mother was out working. She was a maid, of course. And he brought the table back every evening without her knowing. Finally, a British man started coming to the chai stand every day. He would order chai and quietly write in a notebook. He turned out to be a famous writer and wrote about his experience at the chai stand in a popular travel magazine in England and later in his life story in a book. Can you believe it?" He raised his hands to the sides of his head as if it would explode in amazement. "This humble chai hut became a tourist hot spot for all the *goras* and my client and his father opened up other chai stands, each better than the last. Eventually, he made good connections, immigrated to the UK and America, opening up all kinds of businesses there."

"Chacha, you know you tell stories just like Dadi Jaan . . . so passionate."

He chuckled and wiped his plate clean with a small piece of naan.

Shenachi insisted I eat more than half a naan and the lone meatball that sat on my plate. Flavors danced on my tongue alongside Chacha's entertaining story and I enthusiastically scooped another piece onto my plate.

We had our usual chai on the porch, enjoying the last few days of the crisp evening air before the rising heat would consume it. At the shrieking sound of the neighbor's gate followed by the voice of a girl ushering a car into the driveway, I found the opportunity to ask about the people across the street.

"Are they new neighbors?"

"I don't think so. A lot of the same people still live around here but most people do rent their second and third floors out. Renters are always coming and going, I guess. Your Shenachi would know about newcomers better than me. I just eat and sleep here."

He named a few families and their kids that he knew for certain still lived in the neighborhood, of which I remembered none. He took a long sip of his chai and pointed his cup to the neighbors of interest to me.

"Ghelani Saab passed away a few years ago but his wife and son, Haider, are still there. One generation after another comes and goes." He looked longingly to the door leading to Dadi Jaan's room and took another sip.

We sat quietly, no awkward silences, just two people lost in their memories.

That night I stood at the floating vanity sniffing Dadi Jaan's tea-rose perfume bottles, an aromatherapy session that was becoming my night-time ritual. I made a mental note that the tiny brass bottle sticky to the touch would make a nice aromatherapy pendant. Tousling the waves in my hair one way then the other in the mirror reminded me of those childhood moments I spent posing in front of my mirrored closet, wearing the earrings Dadi Jaan gifted me—still my most prized possession. Here I was, an adult, standing at another mirror, primping, and posing. Had I not changed since? I sniffed at my reflection, loathing my lack of action in the past week. I could have woken up late and done yoga back home too, all while being married to Ameer; no hearts broken and no one let down. I didn't regret time away from work and Mom's scrutinizing pressure but that night, when I finally laid the disappointing day to rest, I couldn't help envying Chacha's client.

Between the slow-moving blades of the ceiling fan, I imagined seeing his client's life projected from a movie reel. A sinewy chaiwalla wearing a chai-stained *kameez*, doing the footwork his father was not strong enough to do. The travel writer waiting to be served a strong cup of chai, struggling to sit on a low stool, his sienna-colored bell bottoms fanning out, a tiny notebook in hand filled with cursive scribbles, too difficult for a chaiwalla to attempt to read. Most of all, I could see the chaiwalla's desire for a better life or even just a different one in spite of his circumstances. I, on the other hand had every resource: my own money, Baba's financial backing if I needed it, paid vacation time, a driver to take me around, and a sketch tablet full of a lifetime of ideas for a passion I'd had since my ears were first pierced at Bejeweled in the mall next to the Orange Julius. I wasn't treated to it either after the piercing even though warm tears rolled down my cheeks and earlobes throbbed. I rubbed them to dull the pain and this caused a terrible staph infection with my lobes needing a re-piercing. By then, I had learned to bargain for the Orange Julius before the probing. In the end, I got the pretty earrings and the treat, but not before all the pain.

"ALL RESTED, HENA BIBI?" Surghum tilted his head to asked.

"Yes," I replied exhaling, all breath and no word.

"Your chacha says you'll meet a friend at Zainab Market or was it at Abid Jewelers? If she hasn't left, we can pick her up from her house."

"No. No, She's on her way. She'll meet me there." I spoke robotically, avoiding eye contact as if he would be able to see the lie of meeting a made-up friend run across my pupils.

Karachi is always a sensory overload no matter how many times you've been here. I thought I'd acclimated over the week to the sounds of motorcycles, car horns, strange smells of sewage mixed with *paan* and baked goods all at once, but it felt all new again.

As we approached Sadr, buildings began to look less modern and more colonial. Finials and steeples would seem out of place if they weren't covered with the same soot that colored the string of postmodernist shoe stores with the faux Nikes in the windows. Surghum began to give me tips on shopping in the area. He cautioned me from giving money to beggars no matter how destitute they looked unless I wanted to be swarmed by more. He told me to haggle for everything, and to stay close to my friend at all times.

He double-parked in front of a line of stores selling Persian-style rugs. Pretending to have gotten a text from *Noreen* that she was in one of the stores, I said a nervous thank you to Surghum and told him I'd call when I needed to be picked up. He warned me to stay safe and I questioned whether I should have taken up Shenachi's offer to send her niece shopping with me. I smoothed my uncertainty with an affirming steady exhale and clung tightly to the familiar comfort of my bag under my arm as if it were a person, and entered a long alleyway dotted with stores leading to more stores. I smiled back at Surghum and gave him a thumbs-up, confirmation that I'd found my friend, and quickly entered a shop selling handmade souvenirs: tiny terracotta pots and rickshaws painted in glittery blues and fuchsias, bejeweled with pieces of geometrically shaped mirrors and beads. As a child these miniature treasures from Pakistan gave my dollhouse an ethnic flair.

I peeked out of the shop to see if Surghum had driven off before leaving the glittery shop, leaving the shopkeeper disappointed. Entering back into the alleyway a blonde woman in a peasant skirt escorted by two scrawny Pakistani boys walked past me with the confidence of a celebrity and her entourage. Her glistening skin and unwashed hair tied in a bun suggested she'd just recovered from the stomach issues that plague many tourists. Maybe she felt well enough to do some souvenir shopping in hopes of making the best of a lackluster vacation to South Asia.

On entering a shop with neatly organized brass and silver jewelry, I found myself getting lost in the hunt for pieces that could be translated to the understated American aesthetic, with hints of earthy natural stones and metals only found here that could still declare it was art made by brown hands from across the world.

Eager salesmen buzzed around and asked if I needed help. In my best Urdu, I told them I was looking for something *khaas*—something specific—and that I'd know it when I found it. It signaled to them that I was a serious shopper and would only buy if I found exactly what I was looking for. I learned the *khaas* sentence from shopping trips with Mom. She could meander quietly in shops for hours without interruptions by pestering salesmen. On occasion, she'd encounter a tenacious young salesboy and ignore him by humming a song, pretending not to hear him, her voice rising in pitch whenever they'd start speaking up. I never once saw that tactic fail.

I picked up every piece that remotely caught my eye, feeling its weight, texture, and shape. Ideas of how each piece would or wouldn't work for Nisa put me in the ultra-focused zone I was intensely craving. Why had I waited this long to go out? The corners of my mouth pulled up into a giddy smile.

I was confident like Mom but not entirely her. I knew the language and mannerisms of Pakistan well enough but I was obviously still a visitor. It was something Karachiites could read about you from one thing or another. For one, no resident of this city would need or want to shop for handicrafts and costume jewelry in this part of Zainab Market, and second, most obvious, we just looked different. My cousins used to say we wore our clothes a little strange, with our *dupatta*, if we wore one at all, tied like a scarf around our neck rather than draped over the bosom. Our shoes never looked worn on account of the neatly paved streets we walked on back home. Here in Karachi, flooding and constant foot and car traffic corroded almost every walkable surface.

Two hours had passed and I'd made my way in and out of dozens of shops through various tunnel-like connections that led to clusters of shops. Upon delivering my *khaas* sentence to a persistent bushy-haired salesboy at a shop that sold shiny silver rings attached to white cardstock with "Made in China" in tiny gold print on the back, my confidence began to slip. The boy looked at me and leaned against the counter to whisper "Lashkar, lashkar" to another salesboy of about the same age with a scar above his lip. Not knowing what the words meant made me both angry and uncomfortable. Sure, I was used to whistles outside the Ranchera Market back home, the blatant stares of frat boys huddling at sports bars, and skaters grazing my hair while slow-rolling past me at the Huntington pier, but I knew how to get away if I felt too threatened. Here men usually had more decorum around women, patiently waiting to get on the next elevator if a lone woman was occupying it or politely scrunching close together to let a woman pass down a narrow aisle at a store or on a bus. But there were the occasional boys who would test their limits with women.

"Where you are from? America? Australia?" the bushy-haired salesboy asked in broken English.

I snapped back an annoyed "Excuse me?" accidentally in English, blowing any chance of them believing I was from here.

"I am curious about you."

"Curiosity kills the cats, Murad," Scar snickered.

I made my way to the exit, but he stood in my path.

"Why you are leaving? I can assist you if you like."

"No, but you can help my husband!" I thundered past him.

Scar peeked out to see that I exited the bazaar alone, without a husband. In my haste to get far away from that shop, I walked a few blocks fairly quickly. With my arms tightly folded, a single tear drop smeared across my temple as I pressed on with deter-mined speed, looking for a recognizable landmark where I could call Surghum to me pick me up.

Like the locals, I scurried across the road not minding traffic and spotted a steeple I'd seen on the car ride earlier. On foot I could see that it was part of an ornate church. I heard the revving up of a shiny BMW blasting Punjabi rap. Its driver lowered equally shiny sunglasses to the edge of his nose to make sense of me when I managed to step into an obvious puddle before making it to the green of the church's lawn.

I found a shady area near the steps and pulled my phone out of my bag to call Surghum. I paused, sucked back my tears and put my phone back in my bag. Feeling defeated and overpowered by two pathetic boys pretending to be men was not how I wanted to end my first day out. Instead, I sat on the steps of what I later learned was the St. Patrick's Cathedral, a major landmark in the city and my sanctuary where I could compose myself and plan an alternate way to end my day.

After two groups of families dressed for either a wedding or a funeral walked around me to get into the cathedral, I left the steps to walk the grounds. After I calmed down, listening to the cooing of pigeons strutting around and fluttering away as I approached, I began to welcome the uneasy thought that I missed Ameer. If we were married and here together, like we planned to be after our honeymoon in the Maldives, I could have called him over to punch those guys' faces in or at least just tower over them and shame them in much better Urdu than I could manage.

When the Cathedral doors closed, I returned to my seat on the cool cement steps. The shopping high was long gone and the thought of visiting another store made me nauseous. It could have been hunger that was inciting the queasy feeling in my stomach but I didn't want to attract any unwanted attention eating at a restaurant alone. While I reluctantly shuffled through Baba's jeweler friends' business cards that I had tossed in my bag, I thought I heard someone calling my name.

"Hena!" I heard it again and brushed my hair away to find the girl I saw the other day from the neighborhood excitedly waving at me. This time, her arms flailed like a drowning victim. Seeing her newly familiar face soothed me. *Someone I knew . . . kind of.*

"Hi, Hena. I'm so surprised to see you here. Sorry, sorry. You don't know me yet, but I know you. I'm Annie, your neighbor." She apologized, catching her breath.

"Of course, I remember."

She held the backside of her tunic tight against her bottom and carefully sat down next to me.

"What are you doing here?"

"I was about to ask you the same thing."

"Well, I was shopping at Zainab Market and came here to take a break."

"You walked all the way here from Zainab Market? By yourself?" Her perfectly arched eyebrows lifted even more.

"Why, is it far? I've been meandering, shopping . . . and you're here by yourself too?"

"Yes, but I work at a nearby tutoring center. I get picked up here after I'm done."

"So, are you going home now?"

"That depends. Would you like me to stay?" She must have noted the desperation in my voice. She shaded her eyes from the sun with a floppy notebook that allowed me to see her big doe-like eyes with sparks of yellow spears that shot like sunbursts from their hazel center. Her whole face smiled into a welcome sign, and an exhalation that I'd been holding in since this morning released from my lungs.

"I would love some company." I told her.

We walked to a *bun kebab* vendor's cart where Annie signaled a thumbs-up and thumbs-down for my approval. I flashed an enthusiastic thumbs-up. She assured me that this was a "hygienic cart" and she wouldn't risk my American stomach to just any street food vendor, miming a wave across her stomach with her hand.

With just a few bites, my queasiness left me. The *bun kebab* was already in the process of digestion thanks to all the walking Annie and I were doing while eating. Like a relaxed tour guide she pointed out places such as the Empress Market and the Bohri Bazaar. Occasionally she asked if I wanted to venture in and shop but I waved her request away, saying I'd done enough shopping, though I had no bags to prove it.

"I hope I'm not keeping you, if you need to get home, I totally understand."

"No, just as long as I get home before dark. Want to get cream horns? I know a great bakery." Annie rubbed her hands together.

For the first time this week, I didn't feel like refusing an offer to eat, and something to awaken my sleeping sweet tooth was entirely welcome. My sudden appetite didn't just show up out of nowhere, it was lured gently by the invitation to eat with someone whose company was so needed. Like *Baba in the tea parlor*, I said under my breath.

"Tea . . . you want to get tea? I know a great tea place nearby too."

"Oh no, I was just . . . well . . . maybe with the cream horn." I accepted.

I told her about how much I loved visiting Pakistan as a kid, mainly because of my dadi and the delicious food and people of course, I emphasized. I threw in my memories of playing cricket with the neighborhood kids to see if she reacted.

"Boys, huh?" She arched an eyebrow.

"There was a boy. I had a bit of a crush on him. It was silly, I was like ten. He taught me how to play cricket. Well, he tried to teach me, anyway. I was terrible at it but he was great." I searched for her reaction.

"I bet he was," she chided.

"Too bad you don't remember his name but do you remember which house he lived in on the street?" Before I could lie, we entered a busy bakery. The scent of yeast and caramelizing sugar about to burn swirled around us. The warmth of the ovens made the bakery womb-like. From the shop across the street, I got whiffs of mithai resting in *ghee* and rose-flavored sugar syrups. It was all deeply nostalgic for me. It reminded me of being fed the confection by Dadi Jaan's hands.

Annie ordered three cream horns and pointed for me to grab a table before the girls in school uniforms got to it. I did as directed by plopping down on a chair and claiming another with my bag that looked strangely like the fluffy croissant in the bakery case that Annie leaned against. Having to secure our seats, I regretted missing an opportunity to pay for our food. She'd paid for it expertly ordering while I stood awkwardly watching. Ironically, her petite stature was an advantage in a crowded city. At the *bun kebab* cart her polite "excuse me" with the addition of "sir" parted the crowd of people who didn't want to crush her, which allowed her to order before them.

I watched Annie stand on her toes to get a peek at her cream horns being placed in paper bags behind the counter. From the back she could have been mistaken for a teenager. Skinny jeans wrapped around her straight-as pencil legs, her tunic fit her perfectly, and the floral scarf around her neck draped across her chest like a Victorian valance. I examined my scarf that hung like a tie down my chest, drawing a visible vertical line between my breasts. I untied the knot in it, splaying the fabric down my chest as if it were extensions to my hair. Annie walked back with two cups of chai and pinned the bags of cream horns with her elbows to her tiny waist. I thanked her and told her that she'd have to accept money for treating me today. Her eyes grew big, though I couldn't imagine how they could get any bigger. I had to remind myself that Pakistani hospitality didn't allow for money talk. To her, I was a guest in her home and to offer to pay for anything was an insult.

"You can pay me back in yoga sessions."

"I'm definitely getting the better deal then."

She clicked her tongue at me and explained, "I practice a few postures that are supposed to relieve headaches. I struggle so badly with headaches. I've always wanted to go to a yoga studio but feel so intimidated by all the professionals."

"I go to a studio back home but I'm no professional. I don't think anyone's judging anyway."

Our conversation was easy and natural. Finding something we had in common with yoga made it more so. We spoke about our most challenging postures and she corrected my Sanskrit pronunciation of them all. I joked about how she should feel free to correct my Urdu as much as needed. We spoke mostly in English with splashes of Urdu, which she always paused to make sure that I understood.

I wanted a natural opening to satisfy my curiosity about her personal life but she continued about her experience working at a financial group and never getting the promotion she wanted, leading her to eventually quit. But I wanted to know if the ring she wore on her ring finger really meant she was married or did it only fit that finger? Was the third cream horn for her husband? Was it that guy—Haider? I found it strange that she hadn't mentioned a spouse, kids, or parents by now. I had told her a bit about Baba, Mom, and Omar but mostly about my adorable nephew, showing her pictures of Zain blowing bubbles. I swiped quickly past the pictures of Ameer and I together at Zain's first birthday.

I only caught that she was wrapping up the last few classes of her education at a university, was studying business, and loved birds or had a pet bird and was somewhere in her twenties. Getting an exact age from anyone in Pakistan was impossible. On my last visit here, I was introduced to two second cousins who, when I asked their ages they responded "We're between 15 and 18."

Annie spoke quickly, the way chatty young girls do, but also clearly like a self-assured young woman. Her jaw often rested on her hand while she combed her long ponytail with the other hand. Her thick black hair with natural auburn hues was highlighted by the fading sunlight that was filling the bakery. She looked typically Pakistani, fine and with symmetrical features, dark hair making her skin appear lighter. But her dusty hazel eyes set her apart from others.

It was getting late and I'd already gotten a text from Shenachi asking if I was ok and an audio text from Surghum asking when he should leave to pick me up. I sent a quick reply that I was fine and I'd text a pickup location soon. Annie noticed and put her half-eaten cream horn back into the paper bag.

"I'll call for an iLift to pick us up."

"Why? I have a driver that can get us."

"If he hasn't left yet, then he'll be stuck in traffic. If I call an iLift car, we can be home before he even gets here."

Surghum was calling and said he was about to leave. Annie whispered, "I'll call iLift." I conveyed it to Surghum and after a few minutes of convincing, he agreed it was safer than two girls waiting to be picked up in the dark. "Please, let your chacha know that I could have been on time if you had called me before the traffic rush."

"Don't worry. I'll take full responsibility."

Annie was already on her phone getting us an iLift by the time I hung up.

"I'm sure I've bored you with all of my work and school talk. I know I talk a lot. Tell me more about yourself."

"I was about to ask you the same."

"Oh, my life's boring. Tell me why you're here in Karachi? If it's not too personal."

Personal? Now I was sure Bushra Auntie's less than discreet conversation with me from the street was in fact heard by all. I hadn't spoken about my breakup with Ameer to anyone. Not with Kristen, Marium, Omar, and certainly not with Baba and Mom. They were witnesses to it, after all, and it needed no explanations, but a reckless need to divulge the details of why and how I called my wedding off knocked at my lips. Instead, I reached into my bag and pulled out one of the two pieces of jewelry I managed to buy at Zainab Market: a beaded Pakistani jade necklace with pastel green lines that wrapped around each bead like green smoke. My heart thumped at showing her the treasure I'd found.

"It's nice." She shot it an unimpressed look.

I closed my fist around it to protect its feelings and pulled out the second piece: a chunky brass bracelet with inlaid geometric mother of pearl pieces that made a floral motif. Tilting her head she assessed, "This one is interesting; a little antique and a little . . . sorry, I can't think of the word in English."

I yelped, "Modern-ish, exactly!"

"You know, you have a perfect smile. Perfect teeth all across." She moved her long fingernails across her restrained smile, a row of crooked bottom teeth sat beneath her thin pink lip. Something I hadn't noticed sitting across from her at the bakery where I'd inhaled my cream horn and she'd picked at hers.

"Thanks." I accepted the compliment.

"So, to answer your question, that's why I'm here. I'd like to possibly turn my passion for jewelry into a business. If that makes sense. Well, that and another reason."

"You're following your passion. That is so great. I'm slightly jealous, you know. And I get your style of jewelry. But, what's that other reason?"

Moments later a zippy compact showed up and we got in. "So, what's the other reason?" I gave her a side glance, signaling she already knew. "I heard a little from Bushra Auntie. I avoid her as much as I can but if she knows something, everyone knows it. You know, you don't have to tell me, it's not my business."

"It's ok, I want to talk about it." I looked down at the key chain on my bag, nervously rubbed it as if raring to get going with what I wanted to share. In hushed tones in the back of the iLift, the highlights and painful details of the past few months gushed out of me and into Annie's attentive ears: Ameer and heartbreak, Mom and Baba, disappointment and shame, the exhaustion of living a life without purpose or passion and knowing that I had the talent and resources to create it if I chose. Finally, breaking away from routine and wanting to prove myself worthy of the praise Dadi Jaan always gave me.

She didn't blink once but nodded periodically. As we turned onto Mausumbe Road, I reached the end of my tale and nervously laughed. She didn't respond except for a slow blink of her round eyes.

Squaring herself, she turned away from me and faced the street ahead, "You were living an unintentional life."

I sat frozen to my seat. It was the most concise thought put into words about my *situation*, words I hadn't been able to formulate myself.

"Yoga at noon tomorrow? Remember, you said you owe me." She winked as I paid the driver in the dark, trying hard to make sense of the colorful bills.

Surghum and Shenachi stood watching through the metal peacock-shaped cutouts on the gate. Their eyes followed Annie as she got out at her house. "Your friend is the Ghelani girl? I didn't know they had a daughter."

Too tired and unsure of how to turn the earlier make-believe Noreen into Annie, I ignored their question, simply smiled and gave them the highlights of my day. Chacha came out to the driveway with the phone pinched between his shoulder and ear. "Here is your princess" he spoke into the phone.

I had a long chat with Baba about my day, adding colorful exaggerations to amuse him. He asked about my friend and I nonchalantly told him that Ghelani Saab's daughter was with me, "You know, your old neighbors from across the street?" Baba paused and stammered, "Yes, of course."

Mom spoke to me briefly in short, strained sentences, obviously still upset. I'd accepted she'd be upset with me for the rest of her life.

Eight

Saadia let Annie in and escorted her to the rooftop. She stuck her mat out at me to inspect, seeking approval on its quality. I gave her a nod. We started with sun salutes to warm up. I corrected her cobra pose by pushing her sharp elbows closer together when the sunlight made her ring sparkle for a second. Now that I had shamelessly told her my life story, I expected her to tell me about that ring on her finger. Impressed with her breath to movement, I complimented her. Into our fifth round, her pale skin appeared pink and her breath labored. We took a break in child's pose and I peeked at her from under my arm. Annie was even thinner than she appeared yesterday. The stretchy black leggings taut against thin legs and oversize white tee-shirt made her appear a mere stick figure. Though I was thinner than I'd ever been before, dropping nearly a pound a week since calling off the wedding, there was always someone thinner to make me feel fat. I never thought there was such a thing as too thin but there she was, Annie; and there was me, comparing the visibility of my hip bones to hers.

When she shifted her weight, her shirt scrunched up exposing a long scar, still pink in places, above the hip bone I was envying. It made me shake off the superficial comparisons and found it more acceptable to compare our stamina. We continued our practice, me correcting her alignment whenever possible and admiring her flexibility at the same time. Breathless and sweaty, we lay in *shavasana* at the end, feeling the humidity in the air settle on our skin.

Annie sat up quickly at the sound of a car horn across the street. "I think he's home." Her head bobbed around to see over the tree blocking her house from view.

"Who, your husband?" I inquired. She clicked her tongue and lay back down without answering.

"So, Haider's your brother then?"

"You know Haider?"

"Well, sort of . . . remember I told you about playing cricket on the street with some kids when I was little? Haider was one of those kids."

She turned to her side, sandwiched her hands and slid them under her head and tonelessly answered, "My big brother."

"Right, that makes sense."

"He's that boy you had a crush on, no?"

I steadied my breath and rolled to my side to face her. "I was ten . . ."

"It's ok. I know he's cute and, I guess, charming sometimes." She rolled onto her back and gazed at the lone cloud above us, "He was asking about you."

All that was missing from this scene were sleeping bags and junk food to make it an all-American sleepover. Except, we had chai and samosas on the rooftop after rolling up our yoga mats.

Annie's skinny fingers poked at her phone—I assumed texts of her whereabouts to her mom since our yoga session and chatting lasted longer than expected. We leaned against the railings and she filled me in on a few of the neighbors. Amongst them was a wealthy family whose son was the neighborhood pot dealer;

a married man having an adulterous affair with his 17-year-old house girl, Bushra, the gossiping widow; and then there was the former drama actress, twice divorced, who had late-night visits from a man incognito, rumored to be a celebrity cricketer. Only one spotless neighbor was mentioned, the Memon family two houses down from us. I assumed our reputation was tarnished upon my arrival: the American girl who practiced yoga on the rooftop desperately seeking attention and whose engagement broke off because . . . fill in the blank to your liking.

"Do you wonder what people say about you and your family?"

"No, not really. Hardly anyone knows anything about me, most neighbors don't even know my name. We're just regular people. We go to work, we have friends outside this neighborhood, we keep to ourselves so no one can say anything about us. In fact, this is the only time I've been to a neighbor's house."

"Hanging out with me might change your reputation."

She waved it off like she didn't care.

"You're not married, don't rumors fly around like crazy about pretty unmarried girls like you?"

"I'm only 23, Hena!" She finally disclosed her age.

"So? My mom's been mentioning marriage to me since she got me my first bra and I live in the US."

'My mom only mentioned it to me once when we visited her family in Sialkot. I guess they pressured her so she pushed me a bit but I promised her I would get married at 25, and no less, to whoever she found suitable but of course, I'd have the final say."

"Has your chacha or chachi mentioned my mom?"

"No, they haven't but they knew your dad."

"My mom's quite old, she had us late too. She has osteoarthritis in both knees. You won't see her out and about much."

Annie's long hair hung over the railing and the baby hair around her face stuck against her skin. Her eyes dimmed and a somber look showed across her face when a white car rolled to her driveway. Haider stepped out of it to unlock the gate. I casually opened my bun to let my hair cascade in big waves down my shoulders the way it magically did after a sweaty yoga session—a thing never to be replicated by intentional styling.

"Hello there." Annie called out with a controlled wave.

He gave her a nod hello. To me, he exaggerated namaste hands, pressed them against his chest and got back in the car.

MAYBE IT WAS THE RISING temperatures, something I ate or the excess of energy from a long yoga session but I couldn't sleep that night. I dreaded sleepless nights. They gave me the space and time to relive arguments. After a round of *I should've said this not that* and other rambling thoughts, a thick eeriness filled the space in my head. I remembered ghost stories Dadi Jaan and Baba used to tell Omar and me in this room. This room was filled with benevolent memories and the residual energy of my dadi's five-times-a-day prayer where no haunting spirits could reside, I told myself, and yet I reached to turn the stained-glass lamp on.

I couldn't call Ameer the way I used to those nights I needed the comfort of hearing someone breathing on the phone with me until I fell asleep. He'd ask if I wanted to sneak out to meet him and I'd laugh it off.

"Alright then, turn to your side and let's go to sleep," he'd say, like he was wrapping his arm around me and just like that I'd wake up the next morning with indentions made on my cheeks from where the phone pressed against it all night. He'd leave a text: *You fell asleep so I hung up. Btw you snore.* Calling him now would be picking a scab I was responsible for. I couldn't relieve his pain, I just selfishly needed his voice guiding me to sleep.

Just then the lamplight flickered and I got a text from Annie.

Thanks for yoga today. Interested in exchanging more yoga sessions for sightseeing or help with jewelry shopping, let me know!

Yes to both. I texted back.

I put my phone down, turned the light off and fell asleep with the resolve to create Nisa, possibly with Annie's help, and managed to scare away the ghosts of memories to another night.

OUR MUSCLES WERE SORE THE next morning and we decided to cut the yoga session short. I showed Annie my collection of ideas for Nisa on my tablet, even read her a mission statement I'd played around with. I relished telling her the finer details and the substantial ideas I had for Nisa, how I wanted to give back to the artisans who would create the jewelry down to the kind of chains I wanted for pendants. She *oohed* and *aahed* at them all but mostly at my PowerPoint skills and marketing strategy. At the end of my presentation, I shuffled the few business cards of gold jewelers Baba had given me, wondering if I should even bother telling her about them.

"Why don't you start with those jewelers?" Annie asked. "See if they carry something similar, if not, maybe they can make it. They can all do custom work. I know you aren't looking for real gold but it's a start you know."

I agreed I needed to begin somewhere. We slipped past Shenachi while she was on the phone for her daily check-in with her son which saved Annie and I unnecessary small talk with her and told Saadia to tell Shenachi I was going out.

"I'll drive us." Annie insisted, so we wouldn't be limited by distance and the whole arrangement of pickup locations. I regretted getting in once she started the car and began racing down the street, and stopped erratically when a van approached, jolting my neck hard. It passed us cautiously, unsure of why it was being given the right of way. Annie adjusted her seat, bringing her body inches away from the steering wheel which she gripped as if readying herself for a race. I braced myself by gripping the arm rest. She accelerated and weaved around a pedestrian carrying a bag of groceries but soon we were stuck in inching traffic. Thankful we wouldn't be hurling down any open highways or narrow streets for a bit, I let out a quiet sigh. She honked her horn unnecessarily, yelled out the classic obscenity "oye! *ullu kay putthay!*" at other drivers, puzzled by her driving. We did manage to safely arrive at Abid jewelers.

I pulled on the locked door of the store and Annie pushed the bell. A bearded man buzzed us into his store, a gallery filled with glass jewelry cases. My skin warmed from the lights in each case that bounced off of elaborate gold necklaces. Annie nudged me to introduce myself. When I said hello and whose daughter I was, his demeanor softened.

"Oh yes, welcome! I was expecting you. How is Mushtiaq? You know your father and I went to college together. He loaned me money to buy my first car. Of course, he made me promise to drive him everywhere he needed to go." He chuckled showing his *paan*-stained teeth.

My focus drifted to the tiny gold balls fringing the edge of an elaborate Cleopatra-esque necklace.

"It's quite beautiful, isn't it?"

"Yes, but I'm looking for something . . . different, smaller and simpler." I said craning my neck while Annie dragged her finger across the glass cases, like searching for a specific word on a page.

"Your chacha messaged me almost a month ago to send him photos of some of our wedding jewelry. I assume he sent them to you? I sent him this one in particular. It's one of my favorite bridal pieces."

Annie's finger stopped sliding and I stopped scanning the cases.

"She's really looking for some simple pieces for everyday wear. Do you have more dainty jewelry?"

He pushed a velveted tray with smaller but equally elaborate bridal jewelry towards us.

"Do you have smaller earrings like small *jhumkay*?" I suggested and yet he pointed out larger *jhumkay*, chandeliers that would fiercely yank on earlobes. Annie rolled her eyes and started moving towards the exit. I nodded no and he continued to point at larger pieces of jewelry.

I backed away from his counter and politely acknowledged, "The gems on those are exquisite but they're still too big. Thank you so much for showing me though. We'll be back."

As soon as I turned my back to leave, he smugly spoke, "So I guess Mushtiaq has already purchased your bridal jewelry elsewhere."

Once we got out of view of the jewelry store Annie started, "What were those? Earrings for elephants?" We both laughed hysterically until our sides hurt our already sore muscles.

"I think he thought small meant big." Our laughter startled a muscular man walking by in a fitted baby-blue *shalwar kameez*. He let out a tiny scream and jumped back and we laughed even harder.

Annie guided me to a chicken wrap restaurant – their logo a cartoon chicken in red and yellow – that she insisted I try. We seated ourselves outside under a red umbrella, giving us minimal privacy on the pedestrian-filled sidewalk. Annie wiped her nose on a tissue from her purse and I wiped the tears from the edges of my eyes, taking care not to smudge my eyeliner which was probably long gone from the humidity in the air. We calmed our laughter, being mindful of our surroundings.

"This is like laughter yoga! HA HA HA HE HE HE!" she imitated the famous YouTube guru, causing us to start up again.

"What's so funny, ladies?" A man's calm voice spoke so close to my ear I could nearly feel his breath. I turned to see Haider. His hand rested on the back of my plastic chair as he slowly unbent to stand tall.

"YOU wouldn't find it funny." Annie scoffed and Haider pulled up a chair next to her. She rolled her eyes the way I did when Omar tried to be charming around my attractive friends.

He respectfully nodded his head in my direction, "*Salaam alaikum.*" My cheeks warmed and I couldn't manage a reply.

"Hena, this is . . . Haider."

"We've met before. Well, ages ago."

He set his folded arms on the table and leaned in as if he were studying my face. "We have? You've changed quite a bit then." I recoiled in my chair thinking of how hideous I was as a child.

I wanted to tell him that he'd changed too but I couldn't say it factually. The only thing I remembered was his steely focus that made me nervous and his intense milk-chocolate-colored eyes.

"Have you gotten any better at cricket?"

"Me? Oh no. The last time I played was . . . well . . . with you." I tensely smiled, making my cheek quiver. It happened every time I tried to contain a full smile, which I was once told by Mom made me look like I had a permanent twitch. Even when I was overweight, everyone agreed I had beautiful beaming smile, but in true form, Mom managed to find fault in it.

"So, all my pointers and tips were never used again?"

"I know, it's sad. All of your professional cricket advice just wasted."

Annie's eyes darted back and forth between Haider and me. When she began to fidget, we broke eye contact and he leaned back in his chair, cradled the back of his head in his hands.

"We forgot to order drinks." Annie pushed back her chair, nearly knocking it over and scurried to the counter.

Haider got up to pull her chair back to the table. His thin gray tee-shirt clung to firm shoulders and a worn leather belt peeked out from under his shirt when he sat back down. I leaned back in my chair, crossed my legs, and tried to balance my dangling sandals on my toes.

"So, do you work nearby or did you know we were going to be here?"

"Annie texted for me to pick the car up here, said you two would be having lunch nearby. She may or may not have invited me to lunch. Plus, I thought it was time I should meet you . . . again."

"That means she may or may not be happy that you're here?"

"She's probably unhappy about it but, hey, I knew you first, right?" He rubbed his stubble, hiding a smile.

Annie came back with the waiter bearing our chicken rolls and a load of French fries smothered in mayonnaise. How I would have indulged in the crispy, creamy mess if it weren't for the handsome man watching me intently. Annie cut her roll in half, placed it in a plastic French fry basket and served it mom-like to her brother.

"You two didn't tell me why you were laughing?"

Annie tried not to laugh with a mouth full of food. She gestured for me to tell the story but my fear that it was only funny to us made me wave her off. Annie's food could be seen going down her skinny neck the way a snake swells having engulfed its prey whole. She tried explaining the scene at the jewelers, with me laughing under my breath in between bites.

Haider arched an eyebrow in my direction and Annie told him, "I knew you wouldn't find it funny. You had to be there." My appetite took a pause at the thought of going to more of Baba's suggested contacts who would most likely ask me about the style of my wedding outfit in an attempt to coordinate the bridal jewelry.

I rubbed the ridges on my fingernails, feeling how prominent they'd become since being here and wondered what vitamin deficiency that pointed to. Annie interrupted the randomness of my thoughts, "What's wrong?"

"Nothing," I answered, brushing my hair away from my face.

"No, really. What is it?"

I gave her a stern look to stop asking with Haider around. Though he seemed preoccupied with his roll and working on finishing Annie's drink.

"It's ok." She mouthed to me.

Haider took another man-size bite and joined in, "Yeah, it's ok . . . whatever that means."

I swallowed hard and figured I had nothing to lose but look more pathetic than I felt. Gathering my hair to one side, I took a deep breath to start, "It's just that . . . Annie, I know you suggested I check out my dad's contacts today but after the 'elephant' bridal jewelry, I don't think I can take it. Having people that know my dad ask about my wedding or no wedding is very uncomfortable." I belted out in one breath.

Haider and Annie stopped chewing to stare at what felt like my nakedness. Pakistani people were private about their personal lives; they didn't talk about the shame of broken engagements. And Annie and Haider weren't Marium or Kristen. Essentially, they were strangers. *I'm crude and pathetic*, I concluded.

Tiny wrinkles relaxed around Haider's intense eyes. "You don't have to do anything you don't want." He spoke softly, his words dripping with compassion, something I hadn't been given before.

"Tell me again why you two are going to gold jewelers?" He paused for an answer and continued, "Annie told me about you wanting to start some sort of jewelry business and the type of jewelry you're looking for. I don't know a whole lot about women's jewelry but I don't think you'll find them at any jewelers."

Annie admitted, "I thought, we would start there but it's true, Hena. What you're looking for is like artisanal, handmade jewelry."

"You need to go to Balochistan. Deep into the Quetta mountains. You'd be wasting your time searching in Karachi. Even if you find something comparable to resale, you'll be paying a lot," said Haider.

"And you won't know who made them. That's your whole thing." Annie affirmed.

I was receptive to the information Haider gave so assertively without me inquiring. It was a characteristic typical of men the world over. Though, I greatly appreciated it in the moment. He starred at me, waiting for a reply, his chin held in his hand making the subtle dimple in it more pronounced.

"Sorry, I'm still processing what you said."

"You need to think about it," Annie agreed, adding her signature "you know", which I was beginning to get used to hearing.

Haider pressed his hands onto the armrests of his chair to push himself up and began to say goodbye. I searched for words to form a sentence: *Bye, it was nice seeing you, thank you for your advice,* or *thanks for showing me how to play cricket all those years ago, thanks for the playful flirting today too but mostly, thank you for the permission to not do anything I don't want to do.* I kept it all in and said nothing as we got up to pay for our food. Haider walked well ahead of us, his presence unwilling to go anywhere but straight, diners scooching their chairs in for him and a waiter teetering a trayful of food maneuvered around him. I thumbed through rupees to make our payment.

"I was supposed to pay for lunch. Annie and I had a deal. Annie, he paid!" I yelled to Annie while she shoved napkins from a dispenser into her small purse.

"It's the least I could do for inviting myself to your lunch."

Annie, unappreciative of the kind gesture, walked out not holding the door for either of us.

"I think I parked on . . . so, we need to go right." Annie spoke to herself.

"You parked? What do you mean, you parked?"

"Stop talking, let me think of how to get back to the car."

"Are you serious, Annie? You drove?" His voice rising but Annie ignored him, walking briskly ahead.

His smooth eyebrows furrowed. "She told me you would drive. What a liar."

"And you believed her? You would trust someone who's never driven in Karachi over her?"

"She said you'd driven in Karachi. I doubted it but she doesn't know how to drive at all. I'm surprised to see you two are still alive."

I tossed my head back to laugh. "I'm surprised too." Annie scowled back at us. Haider was staring at my smile. *Was I doing that quiver twitch again?* His stare moved up to my eyes and he smirked.

"It's over here!" Annie squealed.

Haider shoved the driver seat away from the steering wheel and huffed in Annie's direction but she was too busy sending a text to see his annoyance.

"Hena, it looks like I have to work today. A new student just signed up with me. I feel so bad but do you think we can jewelry search another day?" Annie begged before we got in the car.

"Of course, I understand. You have work."

Haider reached over and straightened Annie's twisted seat belt and pressed its buckle into the latch. Not taking notice, she adjusted the air conditioning vents on her side. Sticking his hand out the window, he gestured for the car beside us to let him merge into traffic.

I tried to compare Haider and Annie's relationship to mine and Omar's. Once Omar got his license, I felt like I had gained a little independence myself. The days when he'd pick me up from school if Mom was running late were my favorite. Seeing him roll up in his blue Corolla in the pickup lane made an ordinary school day into an event. We'd take the long way home, stopping at Friendly Liquor where Omar's friend Basim manned his dad's store. He would give me a small pack of the off-brand Oreos and toss Omar the picante peanuts. The scent of green apple hookah perfumed the whole store. I nibbled on the cookies, walking the cramped aisles of the store. Arabic music softly played in the background while Basim and Omar chatted about whatever soccer game was on the tiny TV next to the cash register.

"Buckle up, bukeroo" he'd say, mimicking Baba's thick accent, though, I don't recall him ever physically strapping me in or even checking to see if I had complied. It was strange watching Haider securing his adult sister into her seat. This was Pakistan though, where grown male friends holding hands or giving each other piggyback rides just meant they were playful close friends and no one would think twice about questioning their sexuality. As kids, Omar and I cringed at seeing Pakistani siblings share the same ice cream cone or give each other cute nicknames. Certain customs that were taboo to us were the norm in this part of the world. Basim was bullied in middle school for having a 'gay' dad because a few kids from school saw his dad greeting his brother with a kiss on each cheek the way most Kuwaitis did. Despite having visited Pakistan throughout my childhood, the mannerisms here relating to love and affection still felt enormously foreign to me.

Annie began to argue with Haider about dropping me off at home first before taking her to work. Haider rebutted that the tutoring center was on the way home and it would be best for Annie to get dropped off first. She insisted it would be fine since she needed to kill some time before her next session but Haider suggested she read a book while she waited for her student instead of making him drive back and forth around town.

A man burdened by the weight of a wooden bar attached to ropes that hung two large baskets of guavas from his shoulder sang out the price per pound near my window, deafening me to what Annie whispered to Haider.

"I don't know if this helps but I can be dropped off anywhere and Surghum can come pick me up. I would hate for you two to go out of your way."

"Annie, I'm going home anyway, right? Don't make me drive all around town." Haider spoke softly, almost pleading with her to be reasonable.

"Fine. Whatever."

Feeling ignored, I occupied myself with sending Kristen and Marium pictures of the Empress Market and the cream horns from yesterday. Each captioned with *@the entrance of the Empress Market* and *I could've eaten three more. Miss you!*

Haider was slowing the car in front of the St. Patrick's Cathedral when Annie opened the door before the car stopped and slammed the door behind herself. I hurriedly called out "see you later, Annie," but she didn't look back, her red scarf flowing behind her waved goodbye for her instead.

Haider pursed his lips to exhale. "Come to the front. I don't want to look like your iLift driver. By the way, I need to stop off at my shop for a few minutes. Do you mind?"

"No, that's fine," I answered looking ahead. Automatically, he slid his hand around my seat belt button as if to make sure it was fastened.

A second later, I sent Annie a text asking if she was ok.

"If you're sending Annie a message, I wouldn't. When she gets like this, it's best to leave her be."

"She didn't even say bye."

"Anyway, I'm sorry on her behalf. She gets dramatic . . . it's what women do, I guess."

"And men, what do they do?"

"They take it."

A faint ticking sound from me flicking the ridge on my fingernail with my thumb filled the awkward silence in the car.

"Is something on your mind?"

"Why do you ask that?"

"You're doing that thing with your fingers. You did it earlier."

I pressed my hands in between my knees to contain them. "I'm that obvious? I'm just thinking about Annie."

"And Nisa, your business idea? You think she won't help you now."

"Umm . . . no." I jutted out my jaw even though I was surprised at his insightfulness and ashamed at my transparency. "She seemed upset. I know I just met her but she's already become a friend."

"I didn't mean to . . ."

"You know what men do? They say a thing and then try to unsay it." My hot words rolled out the way I wished they did at the harassing boys from the market or even when Ameer told me to order a salad at Vincenzo's.

Haider looked blankly at me, unsure of what to say. "I think it's the front seat here, everyone that sits in it has been getting pretty angry with me today."

"It might be the full moon." He ducked his eyes under the car visor to search for the moon in the daylight. "Yes, it might be. That would explain things." His smooth lips parted into a warm smile.

When we hit traffic on an unfamiliar road, he asked me to tell him more about Nisa. He nodded his head in agreement when I spoke about highlighting the jewelry makers and their craft. I was finding it had become easier to talk about Nisa, having had practice with Baba and recently Annie. I'd kept Nisa trapped inside myself for too long and it wanted to be let out to breathe all of its ambitions aloud.

My first revelation for Nisa was to my second-grade teacher during career week, to whom I specified, "I want to be a fashion designer but for jewelry and not clothes." I never really said it aloud after that. When a coworker would complement the way I'd stacked my rings or layered my necklaces, I'd casually tell them, "Thanks, I have fun with it," omitting that it took me 15 minutes to figure out the exact order and placement of each piece. Now, my thoughts on this passion were disclosed to whoever showed interest, with each retelling of my ideas for Nisa more vivid, and each delivery of my marketing agenda more refined.

We parked next to a sea of motorcycles. "It seems like you've given a lot of thought to your idea. I can actually imagine your jewelry in a boutique." Haider stretched his arm around the back of my seat to reach for a small cardboard box. His lean intertwining muscles flexed, leading to a small tuft of underarm hair. While he struggled to grab the box, his close gaze rested on me.

"Seems like you've thought of everything except where to get your jewelry made." He gathered.

"I know, that's where I'm stuck. You mentioned Balochistan earlier and I wanted to tell you that I've read about these villages near Quetta where women make jewelry similar to the way I'd want mine made."

"Oh yeah, people in that region are famous for handicrafts and things like that. There's always a special on them on TV during 14 August . . . Pakistan Independence Day." He elaborated as if I wouldn't understand the significance of the date.

"There was a huge expo last year in Karachi with a lot of vendors from the region. I actually met a guy there from a village in Balochistan, Quetta who was selling jewelry and rugs . . . or blankets maybe, I don't remember exactly. He even arranged a hunting trip for me and a few of my buddies near his village but I didn't get to visit his actual village. Anyway, you should really consider visiting the Balochistan province."

"So, you've mentioned but how would I travel there alone? It would be amazing if I could go with Annie somehow but I'm sure it's impossible."

"Yeah, I guess so. My shop is right there. I'll just be a few minutes." He pointed to a music store next to a string of similarly run-down shops with the names of each business on the storefronts, each name painted in colorful Urdu script with phone numbers in equal size font. His shop's marquee was no different except for Music Shop & Classes written in English for a non-Urdu reader like myself.

I wouldn't have guessed he'd grow up to be a musician. Maybe run a business but not a music shop. Though now I couldn't imagine him in any other profession. I felt a bit like I was spying on him from the cocoon of the car. I watched him from a distance take long decisive strides into his shop, each movement rendered into my mind's camera. Knowing nothing about him other than our cricket interactions made glimpsing the layers of his life, a small thrill, finally getting to know him, an experience in of itself.

Three guys on motorcycles rolled to a stop and parked next to the car. Each one had a slightly newer version of the same bike. Dirt kicked up when one of them pressed his kickstand into place. They began talking about speeds and mechanics beyond my interest or understanding. Fine dust rolled in through my cracked window and I tried to hold back a slight cough so they wouldn't see me. I slipped down in my seat and covered my mouth, attempting to quietly clear my throat. The guy with the newest bike still noticed me and in acknowledgment nodded his head in my direction with the others following his lead, showing smiles beneath their helmets.

Catching glimpses of Haider's figure in the dark shop, I wished I'd gone in with him to avoid inhaling dust. He poked his head out of the shop with his hand shielding his eyes from the sun. Before I could give him a reluctant thumbs-up, his eyes locked on the motorcycle guys, still straddling their bikes. He slowly jogged to the car, opened my car door wider than needed, making the nodding guy back his motorcycle up and allow me ample room to exit. "Come in for a bit," he requested. I followed. We walked towards the store, our arms brushing without either of us stepping away.

It was a cavernous little music shop with maroon carpeting worn thin, dotted with circular holes made by discarded cigarette butts that exposed the gray cement floors underneath. Rickety glass cases with rusted hinges hung on wood-paneled walls, showcasing antique instruments. I recognized the lute and maracas carved with Peruvian designs but I couldn't guess what sound a large tweezer-like instrument would have made. My eyes lost focus when music vibrated the glass cases. A heavy black curtain hung over a small doorway separating the music store from the music class in the back. From behind it, the voice of a man instructed students back to their instruments. Shortly after, the sound of guitar strings being plucked and drum cymbals struck without any particular rhythm and it seemed class was starting.

Haider stood behind the counter helping a customer who was asking for a specific type of guitar string. Hundreds of dusty boxes were stacked up to the ceiling hiding the shelving. Haider carefully extracted a small box without disturbing the rest and handed it to the customer. A guy with long oily hair pulled back the curtain and called out 'Chally' for Haider. I assumed it was his nickname but it was one I had never heard before. Haider looked at me and didn't respond. The guy whistled and finally got his attention. "We need help back here." He motioned and pulled the curtain open, a row of silver rings on his fingers sparkled under the store's only fluorescent tube light which was swaying gently side to side.

Haider gave me what I deciphered to be an apologetic look for keeping me, to which I gave a quick shrug of my shoulders and ventured into the class. Yellow light filled the spacious room where a handful of students of various ages fiddled with their instruments. A boy with a baby face who looked barely ten played a steady beat on the drums, while a man with salt-and-pepper hair adjusted his amp while his guitar teetered on his lap. The guy with the oily hair consulted with Haider over a specific chord a blond boy seemed to be struggling with. In the corner sat a girl in black jeans and a Metallica tee-shirt. She began effortlessly playing "Hello" by Adele on her shiny black acoustic.

Haider mouthed to me to *have a seat* and pointed to an empty chair near two guys sitting cross-legged on the floor, hovering over a harmonium. One was in a khaki *shalwar kameez* with sleeves rolled up exposing randomly placed tattoos, and the other, a full-sleeve Henley too hot for the weather and torn jeans, his boney kneecaps poking out like bulging eyes. From their lips dangled cigarettes, ashes not falling, but effervescently dispersing into the air, flowing into the room from a narrow back door that lead to an alley.

Haider whistled to get everyone's attention while he forced the fingers of the blond student onto the guitar chord. The boy nervously played a tune, vaguely recognizable as "Smells Like Teen Spirit". "Like this." Haider spoke, wrapping his arm around the boy's waist to play his instrument for him.

He played smoothly, pressing firmly and nodding when the chords changed, to make the student take special notice. The blond boy whipped back with a nod of understanding and he took over. The pressure to not disappoint the ardent teacher over his shoulder must have been intense. Haider stared intently at the boy's fingers as he plucked each string, a look I recognized from the childhood cricket games. The look that placed an unshaking trust in you like, *It's just you and me. Now, learn.*

I was afforded another glimpse into Haider's life as I quietly floated around the room watching him make his rounds. He spoke to his students softly, letting their music be heard first over his voice. He asked permission before handling their instruments, handed them back gently, taking care not to let the guitar strap and electric cords get tangled.

When class wrapped up, he proudly held the oily guy's shoulder to announce, "Skinner will be performing at Heat tomorrow night, go see him. Grab a flyer on your way out." He pointed one at the girl in the corner, "And Mehak, there's still a spot open for you. Make it happen this time." Her cheeks flushed in response.

I moved from the doorway to let Skinner by with a music stand. He introduced himself to me as Sikander. Haider interrupted and whispered something into his ear, gave him a half hug,

"See you tomorrow night, man." When I wished Skinner good luck he grinned, pretending to strum the music stand in his hand.

Haider and I made our way out into the daylight.

"Sorry, that took so long."

"That's ok . . . Chally?"

"You caught that huh? It's a terrible nickname."

"What's it mean?"

"It started off as *Chaalees* as in the number 40. You know, from the story of Ali Baba and the Forty Thieves?"

"Yeah, from the Arabian Nights stories."

"Well, some of my friends started calling me *Chaalees* and then it somehow morphed into Chally and stuck."

"I'm sure there's a fun backstory to that name."

"I don't even remember. Anyway, sorry again for making you wait around. We've been short-staffed but then we always are."

"Is it hard to find people who can teach music?"

"Yeah, musicians don't hang onto a job too long. Most of the guys that work with me and Skinner are all trying to make it into the industry themselves and teaching novices instead of performing isn't their jam."

"What about you? Is teaching your jam?"

He looked at me, waiting for me to answer my own question.

"I guess it's obvious, you seem to enjoy what you do."

"I do but I'm no different. I'm looking for the next best thing. I wouldn't mind being a professional musician, signed to a label."

"For the love of the music or money?"

"The money," he said with a straight face.

"Really?"

"I could play for the love of it anytime, anywhere. I could play on my rooftop giving you background music while you do yoga. When you play music for bigger audiences you don't just want their applause."

I sucked at my lips and he added, "You don't like hearing that, most people don't like hearing that because it doesn't sound poetic but it's the truth. Musicians want to make music like artists want to make art but we want to get paid for our creativity just as much."

My head nodded on its own like something inside me understood.

"You can have everything and still want more. Some people call that greedy but I have a desire for more." I watched him speak unapologetically, his hands coming off the wheel and gently cutting at the air then slowly resting back down like he was conducting music. Both of us were ambitious and somewhere society told us we had it good enough, but no matter how good it was, it just wasn't on our terms.

"When my dad and uncles argued over money, my dadi used to recite an Islamic saying, 'Nothing will fill the mouth of the children of Adam except the dirt of their graves.' It was a reminder to them to be content with what they had but if our nature dictated our desire for more, why was it so terrible?" I added.

"Right, exactly, we would be told to control our desires . . . no matter how difficult." With those last words, we let the existential conversation hang in the air.

"Why are you stopping here?"

"To drop you off."

"But I live farther down, across from you, remember?"

"I can't drop you off in front of your house. Your family, the neighbors will talk. You forget you're in Pakistan? You should walk from here. Trust me, it's not worth it."

Having a random guy drop me off wouldn't even be acceptable with my Pakistani-American family back home. It was entirely understandable. Still, I was uncomfortable at what felt like being kicked out of the car. I unlatched my seat belt with one hand and opened the car door with the other. Suddenly, I was pulled back by what I expected to be my slouchy bag or the key chain that hung from it caught on something. Except, it was Haider's hand holding onto my seat belt. "I'd like to see you there." He spoke in a silvery voice, handing me the flyer he had given out earlier to his students.

"Will you be performing?"

"Only if you come."

Nine

I lay in bed lazily through the morning and shooed away Saadia when she pestered me to have breakfast. Mom messaged: *Don't be rude and join the family for meals even if you don't eat.* In other words, *who cares if you eat, so long as you're thin and polite.* What she never noticed was that her lack of sensitivity would only incite in me rebellious cravings, damaging her ultimate agenda. I'd often succumb to a generous order of French fries or an entire row of cookies and immediately follow it by starving myself the next day to maintain a quasi-level of thinness. This time, it didn't unravel my self-worth like it did back home. With oceans between us, her voice came in less clear. Besides, here, I was being satiated by more than food.

In an attempt to keep myself cool from the rising temperatures that were beginning to wilt the gardenia blossoms in their cramped terracotta pots on the porch, I gathered my hair up in a bun. When I caught my reflection in the vanity mirror, I noticed that I looked different somehow; for once, beautiful to myself. Loose strands of curls that escaped being tied up rested on my long neck, my cheeks, sun kissed a little more than usual from rooftop yoga, and a glow that could only be a result of the constant humidity in the air.

Haider's suggestion to let Annie be when she was upset didn't seem to fit our unspoken friendship rules. I wanted to message her to see if she'd help me turn a sluggish day around with a brisk yoga session. Since having Annie's company, lone yoga on the rooftop wasn't calling to me anymore. I would even forgo the practice if she and I could have a more productive day out in a bazaar.

Saadia's sandals slapped the driveway all the way to the gate. I pulled back the lace curtain over the small bedside window to find Annie coming in with her yoga mat tucked under her scrawny arm. I knocked on the window with my knuckle to get her attention and gestured for her to come into the patio.

"You're all ready for yoga." A hint of surprise in my voice signaled I wasn't expecting her.

"Thanks, Saadia, you can go." I shooed Saadia away and she walked backwards, assessing the length of my short robe.

Pulling up the wicker chairs in the patio Chacha and I ritualistically sat on for our evening chai felt strange in the hot light of day.

"If you're not up for yoga today, it's ok. I can come another day."

"No, I'm glad you're here. You seemed upset yesterday. Is everything ok?"

"I'm sorry I was in such a bad mood, you know."

"But why? Was it something I did?"

Her eyebrows squeezed together and she shook her head side to side to answer, "No, no, no, it's just Haider. He can be a jerk sometimes. It's all this other stuff with him and nothing to do with you."

"It's ok. I have a brother too. I get it."

"You're great. I knew you would understand." She got up and gave me a hug with the force of a much larger body.

We both decided to skip yoga. Annie admitted she just wanted to come by to see me anyway. She began telling me all about her new student and an older one, who had an incessant crush on her and how much he repulsed her. We had a few laughs at the expense of her lovestruck student. Then, her face sobered, her round eyes went glossy.

"I know Haider asked you to go to Heat tonight. Are you planning to go?"

"Umm, it's a late-night event. I don't know what Shenachi and Chacha would say about it."

"But you want to go?" She asked as if my answer would crush her.

"Only if you come." I used Haider's line to see her thin lips stop flatlining and her eyes brighten.

"You have to go. Haider wants you to meet Skinner's friend Musa. Have you heard of him? He's from New York."

"Why would Haider want me to meet . . . and no, I haven't heard of him."

"Musa is pretty famous here. He has an urban men's fashion line. I'm sure you've heard of him. Anyway, he's adding men's jewelry to his line. He designs exclusively for men so Nisa would be no competition for him, but Hena . . .,"she squeezed my hands that sat on my lap, "he's the perfect person to network with. Plus, he's known to have a weakness for pretty girls and with your looks he would give you every detail of the business."

"He sounds like the right person to meet but . . ."

"Hena. I'll go with you. Tell your chacha you're going to the Heritage Night Fair at the university, everyone knows about it. Tell them, after that, you'll be having dinner with me and my friends at Port Grand to celebrate my birthday."

"Wait, that's a lot. First, do you really want to be around your brother today? And, I want you to go if you want to and not to help me network and . . . what, it's your birthday?"

She laughed, "No, it's next week. As for Haider and me, we're always fighting about something. He gets these big ideas and I tell him to be sensible. Of course, he's a man and doesn't want to be told what to do and so we argue. Anyway, he usually does what he wants."

Dusting her hands off, she concluded, "The end. I'm used to it."

Chacha tried to discourage me from going out at night but Shenachi was desperate to have her son's visit be just the three of them. "I've been to the Heritage Fair with Khalil plenty of times and it's a safe family outing. In fact, most of the people from the neighborhood are planning to attend. It'll be fine," she told him.

Chacha's eyelids drooped the way Baba's did when he was worried but he declared that I could go on the condition that "Surghum will drop you and your friend off and pick you up . . . no iLift!" He wagged his finger uncomfortably close to my face.

I agreed and rushed off to send Annie pictures of suitable outfits for me to wear. My only cool cousin had once told me and Omar about elite Pakistani nightclubs with full bars, private booths in the back, and scantily dressed girls. He touted that these clubs riveled those in Dubai, a country he'd spent a summer partying in.

I hadn't brought anything remotely trendy or sexy with me from home and when Annie vetoed every outfit, my frustration began to brim into panic. Instead, Annie made up her own strange combinations, suggesting a long skirt paired with a shirt tucked in would be stylish. She quelled my anxiety when she mentioned that Heat, despite its name, had a more 'chill vibe' with a musician friendly atmosphere but her outfit choices for me still seemed nun-ish.

I decided on my go-to skinny black jeans with a black silk spaghetti string camisole that was actually part of a PJ short set, perfect for sleep on hot nights. I'd thrown on a thin knee-length shrug when leaving the house for modesty's sake in front of Shenachi and Chacha. It looked silly buttoned up to my neck, hiding the layers of my favorite brass chains and geometric pendants, but it wouldn't jeopardize me being able to go out.

"And we have to go with Surghum?" Annie questioned for the third time. Something about him reminded her of a pervy uncle she hated. I kept the interaction between them nonexistent by keeping Annie engaged in conversation. She spoke to him once, giving him the address to enter into his GPS, which he never used and proudly insisted he knew the roads by memory. Everyone in the family knew that Surghum couldn't read. Not English, nor Urdu. It was the reason he always sent voice texts and often called to get pickup locations.

It was hard to make out in the car, but it seemed Annie was wearing a dark maxi dress that was swallowing her tiny figure. The slit up the side of the dress showed patent leather knee-high boots instead of any leg.

From time-to-time Surghum stopped humming and snuck suspicious looks at us in the rearview mirror. When we arrived near the floodlights of the fair to walk the rest of the way where cars couldn't enter, I thanked Surghum. As usual, he warned me to be careful, narrowing his eyes on Annie.

"See, I told you. He's weird," Annie remarked and I laughed, aware of Surghum's harmlessness.

Moments later a zippy iLift showed up to pick us up and we drove off to our actual destination. The driver tapped his thumbs against the steering wheel in rhythm to an 80's Pakistani song full of electric keyboards and the soft voice of Junaid Jamshed.

Without the daylight exposing the trash-scattered streets and pools of stagnant water in potholes, the city glittered only with tiny lights, masking imperfections and transforming people on the streets into sleek, black shadows. If I was ever out at night in Karachi, it was with Mom on frantic last-minute shopping trips before our flight, Surghum driving us terrifyingly fast so we could get back home to pack and head for the airport. I'd only witnessed Karachi's nightlife through the bug-splattered windshield that blotted the sharpness of the city of lights into vague smears.

With Annie as my cohort and the iLift driver slowly cruising, obviously lost in his music, I could take in each source of light that winked at me. There were vintage Edison light bulbs strung from every street vendor's cart, neon signs buzzed on storefronts, fanned-out light dispersed from half-moon-shaped shades that hung at the top of weathered billboards. Then, there were lights that lined a promenade like a runway, almost in reach of the sparkling lights of the marine ships on the murky Arabian Sea. Layers of light over light, even the moon swimming in orbit over us but not competing with the magical opulence of manmade light in a crowded city.

The driver pulled his car halfway up onto a low sidewalk of a dark street lined with mechanic shops, now mostly closed. The only light illuminating the street at all was under a street lamp that revealed the otherwise invisible specks of moisture always in the air. Under it was a small chaiwalla's cart. Steam from his cauldron rose up through the partly opened lid creating the illusion of a much cooler night.

No sign of a club. Annie pushed to get out and led me down a much darker alleyway maneuvering around puddles with the bottom of her dress in her hand. We approached a flickering blue tube light that sat over what seemed to be the back door to the club. Annie knocked rhythmically and Skinner appeared, to let us in. He looked us up and down, seemingly by our wardrobe choices. He opened another door, blasting us with blaring music.

"Give us a minute," Annie yelled as he left and the door latched shut; the music fell silent behind the heavy door.

"You look plain. Here, put some kajal on!" She shoved a nubby cone-like eyeliner to my face, an almost ancient makeup product that I'd only ever seen sitting on Dadi Jaan's vanity. Annie stopped me short of the liner touching the rim of my eye and quickly wiped its tip with the edge of her dark dress, staining it forever. Without a mirror, I felt for my lower lid while I watched Annie shed her dress, revealing a tight mini-dress, white with a red line running down one side, making her look like a Swiss flag.

Speechless at her transformation, I slowly attempted to unbutton my shrug. Annie shoved her dress and, in one pull, my shrug into a fabric tote. Her thin long fingers pressed hard trying to wedge it into a corner next to a bucket and box full of broken wires.

"Ok, that's better." She assessed me and expertly swiped the eyeliner in the rims of my eyes.

"I thought you said this was a 'chill' club. I should've worn something else. You were trying to get me to dress like a nun earlier."

"You're fine, you look mysterious. You'll always stand out over me, anyway!" She pulled me into the noise of the club.

My body stiffened when Annie insisted we walk through a crowd on the dance floor instead of going around them.

Loosen up I thought she said but I couldn't read her lips over the music. I hadn't been to a club since Marium's birthday over a year ago when I felt secretly uncomfortable the entire night. When Ameer showed up, I clung to him, giving him the impression I was more into him than I was.

A year later, across the world, the same globalized scene played on, with me feeling out of place. "Stay here, I'll be right back." Annie pointed to the floor next to a pillar. I grabbed her arm like I was being dropped off at kindergarten for my first day of school. Unloosening my grip on her, she assured, "I promise, just one minute." I watched her exaggerated gait move past Skinner who hunched near a small stage, sucking on a hookah pipe.

I replayed Annie's "You'll always stand out over me" sentence that matched Marium's "You bitches better not look hotter than me on my birthday!" the day we went shopping at a favorite Laguna Beach boutique for something to wear to her birthday bash. Kristen and I insisted we couldn't if we tried but made sure we didn't outshine our friend with the tough-girl exterior who was as insecure inside as the rest of us.

In spite of my disgust at the couple dry humping in the corner booth and my concern for the group of friends doing way too many shots at the bar, I nudged myself to at least observe the experience of being in a fairly entertaining place without judgment. When Skinner spotted me, he held up his hookah pipe up as invitation to come over. I made my way around two tipsy girls in micro minis who were knocking over amber-colored drinks when two overly groomed men cut me off to narrow in on them. Before I could continue to make my way to Skinner, an underdressed man in a slouchy denim shirt approached. American, I guessed.

"I'm Musa. I've been sent to meet you." A slight Pakistani accent could be picked up when he spoke.

"I'm Hena, and they warned me you'd come."

He laughed freely, like an uninhibited American, and complimented. "But they didn't tell me you were stunning."

My smile weakened at his flirtation. Musa was certainly handsome but I was never comfortable with compliments. He gestured for us to sit at a table that was occupied by an elegantly dressed couple. They got up to congratulate Musa on his new line and left for the bar.

"You have a new line of jewelry, right? How exciting. Congrats." I leaned in to speak instead of shouting over the music.

"Thanks! It's taken a lot of patience. I've gone over my own deadline three times. Everything moves a lot slower here as I'm sure you've gathered."

"So, Annie says you live in New York. You must go back and forth a lot."

"I've been stuck here for six months. I just don't want to leave until the launch but I'm so freakin' homesick." He leaned in, resting his elbow on the table and studied my eyes. His long lashes vibrated from the thumping music. "How about you? How long have you been away from home?"

"I haven't been here long enough to get homesick; leaving in less than two weeks."

"Skinner's friend, that chick with the go-go boots, said you were trying to set up a business or start a line . . . sorry, I didn't get all the info. I just saw you standing there looking lost and, don't mind me saying this, but I thought you're sexy as hell and I'd let you explain it to me yourself."

I'd dated his kind before. He was bored and wanted to play for a while, never the pretense of a relationship. Handsome, rich, came with a side of useful connections. The latter, of interest to me.

"Go-go boots gave you all the info. There's not much more to it." I started modestly describing my vision for Nisa: a socially conscious brand, then leaned into the intricate parts of my designs, stressing that I wanted everything handmade. He listened, his attention entirely there, eyes unblinking in the same manner as Haider. *Did all young Pakistani men share this steely focus?* I fiddled with my fingers, trying to read if my little nonexistent Nisa would be brushed off by an established designer or if my globally conscious idea touched a softer part of his entrepreneurial soul. His legs opened wide when he leaned in to rest his elbows on his knees and asked for my number without looking up from the phone in his hands.

"Sent you my number, call me tomorrow. I'm going to be at my studio in Clifton. It's going to be a busy day so if you don't mind talking between meetings, we can formulate a plan for Nisa." He added, "But there's no way you could leave in two weeks. A brand doesn't jump from idea to product that fast. Plus, I'm just getting to know you."

We exchanged demure smiles. Feeling cool on the inside, I ignored the nagging voice that asked what Musa would want in return for his help. The DJ stopped the music and introduced the club's live music segment, with Skinner performing first. I turned away from the stage to see Musa offering Annie his seat.

"I'm guessing from that smile you were able to charm him."

My irritability with Annie dissipated and Heat didn't bother me anymore.

Skinner pressed his lips against the mic skewing his voice, "This song is dedicated to a girl wearing black tonight" A cheer went up from all the females in the club. Besides Annie, almost every girl wore black. Annie shrank in her chair. Skinner sang an Urdu ballad with ear-piercing riffs of the guitar. Haider peered out from behind the stage at the end of the performance and shot an annoyed look at Annie who was cheering for Skinner obnoxiously loudly.

Three other bands played covers for popular American tunes and did far better at their own original pieces. Mehak, the guitarist from the music class nervously sat on a tall stool shielding her eyes from the spotlight. She played another Adele song on her acoustic guitar. While she played, Haider quietly pulled up a chair next to me. My heart fluttered when he whispered, "You're here. I guess, I'll have to perform now."

The DJ introduced 'Chally, Of Chaal Chalak!' and Haider left my side, his black shadow moved smoothly towards Mehak to give her a high five. The spotlight changed color from white to a smoky red. Moments later Haider appeared on stage. Girls hooted for him as he slid the stool in between his legs, gently placed a blue-and-white guitar on his lap, and carefully adjusted the mic to meet his mouth. After scanning the audience, he stopped at our table to speak, "I wasn't supposed to perform tonight but I promised someone I would. So, here it is."

I didn't take him for a singer but his voice rasped at the right spots and trilled at others.

Two lost souls swimming in a fish bowl, year after year. My voice sang quietly along with him to the Pink Floyd song. Long after the applause ended, I kept swaying to the music playing in my head.

The spotlight on the stage dimmed, the DJ pumped his music up again and called everyone to the dance floor. Annie's eyes flashed with excited enthusiasm and I gave her a big 'no.' I asked her to point me to the bathroom and her finger danced its direction to me. We both left the table, Annie shuffling her way into the crowd on the dance floor, and me making a U-turn at the bathroom to find Haider and Skinner near the stage, now crowded with girls. Mehak was zipping up her guitar case in the corner when I approached her like a groupie.

"You were amazing! Hi, I'm Hena by the way. I saw you yesterday at the music class."

"Thanks."

"How long have you been practicing with Haider?"

"Who?" She looked at me confused.

"Haider . . . I mean Chaal Chalak, is it?'"

"He goes by Chally. He's been working with me for a couple of months but I started with Skinner two years back."

"That's awesome. What's it like being the only girl in the class?"

"I'm the only girl in this particular class but there are other girls who take other classes at the music shop. Anyway, what does my gender have to do with anything?"

"I guess, nothing. Are you heading out now?"

"This is not my type of venue. I just did it to get everyone off my back. Everyone here is either trying to get laid, get drunk, or perform for a lame crowd."

Before I could nod a dorky *I totally agree* and have her give me a teen-angst sneer, Musa comically interrupted, "A thousand pardons."

Mehak swung her guitar case over her shoulder, glared at him, and stomped away.

"Would you like to join me and a couple of my friends for camel rides on the beach?"

I tapped the bow of my lips and inserted, "If I wasn't in Karachi, I'd think it was code for something more risqué."

"That could be arranged. But this is just a few of my artist friends." He pointed to two guys wearing head-to-toe patterns and a tall girl with fluffy blonde curls dressed similarly to me, congregating at the bar. "They get pissed drunk and attempt to mount and sometimes manage to stay on top of the camels. It's actually pretty hilarious."

"You seem quite sober though."

"Well, you have to be a sober spectator to find the absurdity hilarious. Plus, I don't drink and something tells me you don't either. We can laugh at them together and possibly judge whether our sobriety is less or more fun than their drunkenness."

Annie took a break from dancing to rub her feet from outside her boots. In earshot of our conversation, she gave me a thumbs-up to accept his invitation. Skinner jumped into the space between Musa, nearly knocking him over with a bear hug. Haider walked past them, bumping my shoulder hard enough to jolt me forward, causing my hair to cover my bare shoulders like a shawl.

"I need to talk to you," he spoke into my hair and walked off looking back for me to follow.

"I'll be right back . . . maybe, take a rain check on that camel thing?" I patted Musa on the shoulder while he tried to break away from Skinner's aggressive embrace.

Annie appeared in the corner of my eye, cutting through people in conversation to get to Haider before me. She pecked fiercely at him in rhythm to words I couldn't hear. Her arms flew around as she spoke and he showed her the palm of his hand to stop.

I sped up to hear the content of their argument and only caught a few of her seething words "I can't believe you, Haider, you just don't care at all!" She looked back at me with teary red eyes, "I'll meet you in the change closet in 15 minutes."

"Annie!" I started after her but she turned back and begged, "Please, I need to be alone."

Haider called for me and opened the door that led us outside into a misty alleyway.

"What's happened? She's really pissed."

"I don't want to talk about that." He rubbed the back of his neck struggling to find the words. "That guy Musa you've been talking to. You should stay away from him. He's got a crazy reputation and I heard he's married to some white woman in the US."

'What? I should . . ."

He interrupted, "You think he's going to help you with your jewelry business because he's famous or whatever but he's just baiting you. There are other people and ways to get your business started."

"Like who, Haider? I'm only here for two more weeks and I haven't gotten anywhere."

"Like me. I'm from here." He tugged at his shirt's neck and blew his breath down his chest to cool off. "You may think I run a crappy little business but I know what a business takes. It takes regular people to make it work. Not fancy designers making millions on the effort of sweatshop workers. If you want Musa to help you make a huge brand, maybe he could do that but I'd hate for you to lose sight of what you want to do, what people with good intentions want to do here in Pakistan . . . and I'd hate to see you with someone like him at all." Scrunching his broad shoulders, he shrank away. I stood speechless, shifting my weight from one leg to the other.

"You would take me to Balochistan?"

Ten

From the rooftop I could hear the snack man's lyrical call stop short on the street. Bushra auntie's heavy voice instructed him to give her the fresher-looking figs. He argued that they were dried fruits and one bunch wouldn't be fresher than the other. Still, she insisted and he held up a darker bunch strung together on a hemp rope that she accepted. The same kind Dadi Jaan would get me, knowing I wouldn't eat them but would wear them on my wrist like a chunky bracelet.

I stretched my legs out and attempted a deep bend to reach my toes, deciding not to let another day lapse without exercise. Holding the posture I hadn't practiced in weeks created new tension in my lower back. I held it longer, telling myself that I wouldn't release my toes until the snack man's creaking cart started down the street again. I took deep breaths through the challenge, wishing the snack man would roll away and allow me sweet release. At the sound of Annie's giggle, I blew away a curl of hair obstructing my vision. Haider was at the snack cart, watching the snack man scoop roasted peanuts into a black plastic bag, not in the newspaper cones I'd seen Baba eating out of in the sepia-colored photographs from his youth.

The snack man's call sluggishly echoed as he made his way down the street. Haider popped a peanut in his mouth and wrapped his arm around Annie's neck to pull her head into his arm. It was a relief to see the siblings' dispute from last night had blown over. The cause of the conflict was still unknown to me as Annie had sat silently in the car on the way home with Surghum giving us his suspicious looks.

Annie broke away from Haider's headlock and ran across the street to join me for yoga. He held up his hand shading his eyes from the sun, gave me a nod before walking through the gate of his house. While he appeared calm as usual, nervousness rose in my stomach at being instructed to not tell Annie that I'd be meeting with him later in the day.

Annie's doe eyes puffed around the lids like she was recovering from an exhausting night of drinking or possibly crying. I had done neither but I too showed some wear from the late night out. Shenachi had given me a side glance this morning when I said *salaam* to her, accompanied by a yawn, and trudged up the stairs.

Annie followed my queues with a short stretching session. I would have prodded Kristen to tell me how she was feeling after witnessing her have an emotional blowout like Annie did last night, but if Annie didn't want to explain her spikes in mood followed by her cold silence, I wasn't going to pry.

"So? Are you going to meet with Musa sometime?" she prodded me instead.

"Maybe, I'm not sure yet."

"I can tell you are kind of sick of me. I'm sick of myself too. I just get so angry." I deliberately turned away from her into a twist. "I had another argument with Haider. He didn't want me to introduce you to Musa. He doesn't like him very much and I said something stupid to him or called him stupid, I can't remember. It's just that we're all we have, and we know how to push each other's buttons so well, you know." Wilting in the afternoon heat, her tiny frame looked helpless but something about her explanation didn't match the intensity of her rage with Haider.

"I have a brother too but you and Haider still live together, share a car and responsibilities. It can all be too much. I get it but why did you tell me he wanted me to meet Musa when he didn't?"

"I was hoping it would persuade you to meet him. I think Musa's perfect for you and Nisa, of course. It looked like you two hit it off too. I saw you guys were making bedroom eyes at each other." She snorted a laugh.

"You *think* you saw that. Anyway, I do think he could really help me get Nisa going and, at the same time, I just don't feel comfortable with him, like he's going to want something for his help."

"I don't know, what if he wants to help you because he likes you? Well, whatever you want. I won't push you anymore." She pressed both hands in my direction signaling a stop. "I have some time today, do you want to go to another bazaar?"

"No, not today. I have to visit my thia later."

Escaping from the heat and humidity that was intensifying every day, I jumped into a cold shower after seeing Annie out. Like icy fingers, water streamed through my hot scalp. It awakened my mind and soothed the restlessness I was feeling about my task here. Possibilities and opportunities for Nisa were beginning to manifest. At an awkward night in a noisy club, I met a successful man who could expertly guide me through the workings of a business I'd dreamt of having all of my life. In the same night, I'd been offered the steady hand of my childhood crush, who could cut through the bull and help me keep Nisa's integrity on its purposeful path.

I readied myself to meet Haider in a confident, calm frame of mind, tucking a loose gray tee-shirt into my most comfortable jeans, the ones with the small tear on the thigh that I had hesitated wearing here because a little skin would peek through if I stretched my leg a certain way. I poked my most prized pieces—Dadi Jaan's delicate gold and turquoise earrings—into my ear lobes. When I lifted my damp curls off my neck to give them a glance, they bounced with the same enthusiasm as the first time I placed them against my ears as a little girl.

"I hear you're going back to the university today for some lecture. If you like it, you could enroll here."

Chacha had taken the day off and with Shenachi busy making preparations for the renters to move in upstairs, he was bored and wanted my company over a cup of chai on the porch. Surghum was just beginning to rinse the suds off the car which meant we had ten minutes, not nearly enough time to let the scalding hot chai cool to a drinkable temperature. Haider's text vibrated in my hand *Have you changed your mind about meeting today?* I replied, *Running a little late, be there soon,* and shot Surghum a hot glance for insisting the car needed to be washed. Chacha and I sat in the squeaky wicker chairs, me cooling my chai with big bellows of breath. Chacha was already slurping his, not minding the burn.

"One of these days you should visit Thia Kuli and your cousins. Your baba didn't press me to take you but I think it would be a shame if you didn't at least drop by to see them."

"Wouldn't that be awkward?"

"What do you mean?"

"I just figured it wouldn't be appropriate if Baba and you aren't really speaking to him."

"Who said I'm not speaking to him? I just saw him last month."

"I didn't know that."

"He's my brother, Hena. I know he's not perfect or rather he's influenced by his wife but he has rights over me and rights to this house too. Your dad forgets that sometimes."

Though Baba never filled me in on his family's politics, I was a witness to Dadi Jaan handing Baba a stack of legal documents, including the deeds to the house. It was the same day she displayed her jewelry out on her bed for me to take my pick. Which meant I couldn't resist speaking up about it now.

"Chacha, I don't know all the details but I do know Dadi Jaan left the house and any decisions to be made in regards to it to Baba. I'm sorry, but I was there the day this happened." I spoke with confidence, taking a long sip of my still-too-hot chai.

He sat slack jawed for a moment then spoke, more softly this time. "You remember all that? You know more than I thought. Hena, your dad was the favorite and you're right, he has been left in charge and we should abide by his wishes. He wanted us to rent the upstairs space and we did, right?" he asked. It was true that I did know more. I knew Shenachi and Chacha wanted to save the upstairs for their family. Now that their son had a steady job, he would soon marry, bringing his wife to live close enough for Shenachi to keep an eye on—all while giving the young couple their space upstairs, creating the classic extended family structure of living under one roof - almost holy amongst South Asians. I was also aware that Baba would be furious if he knew Chacha was fraternizing with Thia Kuli and, who knows, possibly scheming against him.

"Car is all ready for you, Hena bibi," Surghum yelled from the driveway, tossing a dirty rag at Saadia to throw away for him.

Through the side of my eye, I took notice of Shenachi's floral-print *kameez* through the crack in the door where she secretly stood listening to our conversation. Chacha stopped me before I made my way inside to grab my bag and return the chai cup to the kitchen.

"And, Hena, don't tell your baba I've been seeing Kuli. I want to tell him myself. These things have to be handled carefully. You understand, right?" His plea pained me but I took advantage of the opportunity to grab my bag and hurriedly tell him that I'd be going on a short sightseeing trip to Balochistan.

"That's very far and I don't think your baba would approve and with whom will you be going?" His concerns needed to be quelled quickly.

"With my friend from across the street and her brother and possibly an official tour guide if he has room for us in his group. I'll talk to Baba about it today and I'll tell you the details this evening." Lifting his arm limply to wave bye to me, I quieted his worry, "I won't tell Baba about Kuli. It's not my business. You can tell him." Before the gates closed on the driveway, I waved to Shenachi, still hidden behind the door, letting her know I was aware of her spying.

THE TEMPERATURE MUST HAVE DOUBLED by the time I got to the university grounds. When I got out of the car, my tee-shirt stuck to my back. A typical ornately decorated Pakistani bus blew exhaust fumes towards me, billowing my shirt and causing it to peel away from my body, giving me some relief. I reread Haider's text about where to find him on the campus grounds. Every tree was occupied by studying students who took shelter under the fleeing shade. Haider was lying under the largest tree, taking up more room than he needed; a group of girls on the less shady side held up books to protect themselves from the penetrating sunlight. Making my way to him, I watched the heat exuding from the ground blur the scene, making him look like a mirage.

"I was just about to leave. Thought you decided to take Musa up on his offer instead of me." As he spoke, his arms covered his eyes. I knelt down next to his head, my hair brushed his arms and he shot up. His eyes examined my hair blowing around my face in the hot air.

"You know you have a staring problem?" When he didn't respond, I elaborated. "You stare . . . at me. I can't tell if you're amused or disgusted."

"Does it make you uncomfortable?"

"I'm not sure." I tousled my hair to one side to match his stare. "You're doing it again!"

"Then I don't think I know I'm doing it. I was just looking at you."

"I guess you staring doesn't make me as uncomfortable as not telling Annie about us meeting today. I mean, if we're going to take her with us why can't she know? And I know it's not any of my business but why was she so upset with you at Heat?" When he said nothing, I stammered on nervously, "I am very grateful for your help but I have a lot of questions before I make travel plans anywhere."

He jumped up and dusted dry pieces of grass from his pants. "Do you think we can get something to eat before all these questions?"

We made our way to his car, and again he made sure my seat belt was securely on before starting the car.

"That. Why do you do that?"

"It's a habit. Just something I've always done. Burgers and fries, the classic American fare ok with you for lunch?"

"Pakistani fare would be fine too. Whatever you want."

He sauntered into a nearby restaurant, leaving the car running and AC on for me. Eating fries by the handful, he pointed out streets that led to other music shops in the area. When I smelled the salty ocean air, he pointed out the salt flats' blinding white patches. Two thin men were hunched over, tending to the salt, their bare feet ankle deep in tiny pools of water, their skin almost black from working next to the reflective ocean.

Haider stretched his arms wide as if to hug the atmosphere. A softness appeared on his face, freeing the cool stoicism that usually presided over his face. He led me to an alcove on the beach where we settled, kicking our shoes off to the side. The crashing waves provided a kind of background music and we didn't say much other than 'ketchup?' or 'get the tissues!' when they nearly flew away. He anchored them with my phone. I tied my hair up in a bun to stop myself from taking bites of it with my burger.

"The reason I didn't want to tell Annie about us meeting today was to give us time to plan and sort things out for the trip without her hysterics. We've been at odds lately and I don't know if you noticed but she's a bit jealous of you and me getting to know each other."

I had noticed Annie's eye rolls the day we all had lunch together, the strange silent treatments, and her pushiness for Musa and I to meet. Maybe she wanted to get a heartbreaker or at least an engagement breaker like me away from her brother.

"Annie and I are close. We've always been but she takes it to another level with wanting to get into my business. She's protective when she sees me talking to a pretty girl, especially one of her friends."

"It would be a little weird for me too if my brother was flirting with my friends."

"I didn't say I flirted with her friends, just talked to them."

I didn't bother asking him to tell me the difference. Both of us stared out at a fisherman and a little boy on a paint-chipped cobalt-blue boat floating on the gray water.

"Why were you and Annie fighting at Heat?"

"Her dress. It was inappropriate. I told her and she flipped out. What else do you want to know?"

"If Annie's threatened by you and me, which is absurd, how is she going to agree to go on this trip with us? She has to go with us. My family is not going to let me go with you alone."

"First of all, why is the idea of you and me absurd?"

"I mean we don't really know each other."

"It's fine." He scooted away from me as if to protect his pride. I inched in closer to let my body language speak for me, that the idea of him and me was not insane at all and very much in my coherent thoughts.

"She'll go with us. I know she will. I can convince her."

"She told me you always get your way. I guess she was right. If this trip actually works out, it would be great to celebrate Annie's birthday there. Hey! That may give her incentive to go."

When he didn't respond and lost eye contact, I assumed he'd lost interest in the topic. I realized too late that his eyes were actually on my phone's screen, displaying a text from Musa that read: *I was looking forward to seeing you today. What happened?*

Haider did a tight shoulder circle and offered me his hand to help me up.

"Annie would like that, a sort of birthday business trip. Quetta is one of her favorite cities too. Come on, let's walk and talk."

"I really want to discuss money. I know Pakistani people hate talking about it with friends but you're going to be taking time off from your shop so I insist on paying for the trip expenses." I spoke without pause. His eyes bugged out the way Annie's did at the mention of me paying for our cream horns at the bakery but I pressed on. "I won't go if we don't work this out, Haider. I mean it."

"Ok, ok. Annie can be in charge of money matters. It'll make her feel important."

In the alleyway outside of Heat, Haider had already explained that we could meet with Shabaz, an acquaintance he'd made at the Pakistan Day Expo. Shabaz was the Cultural Development Attaché for his small village of Balandi which sat on the outskirts of the city of Quetta in Balochistan, nestled in the snowy mountain ranges. Besides what the village earned from game hunting and weaving wool rugs, the women of the village were contributing by making traditional jewelry, a skill passed down to them for centuries. It was exactly what I'd read and reread about Balochistan's remote villages in Global Magazine. Shabaz had confided to Haider that he was basically giving the jewelry away at the exhibition and, even then, wholesalers wanted a better price for an art that was slowly dying and needed preserving.

Could it be serendipity, decreed by the divine, that what I was seeking was also seeking me? A part of me felt undeserving of the goodness being laid at my feet. Hadn't I broken Ameer's heart? Hadn't I shattered Mom and Baba's hopes for me? Most of all, hadn't I been an inactive participant in my own life, letting years go by without taking a stab at Nisa?

"Have you had a chance to talk to your family about the trip?"

"I mentioned it to my chacha before I left. I told him the same thing we discussed yesterday. I just don't want their involvement in it yet. I'll just be sightseeing the Balochistan province to them." Maybe, Baba would understand that the jewelry I wanted couldn't be made in Karachi, that it was rustic and one of a kind. Certainly, he would agree with the benefit of buying from the source instead of a price-gouging middle man. Still, if he knew I wanted to go on this trip solely for Nisa, he would insist Chacha take me. That would inhibit and hinder me in every way. In keeping the trip's motives to myself, I could also preserve my ego that cautioned, *if things didn't work out, no one else would have to know.*

I felt confident I would be with two Karachiites with a Balochi attaché on the other side expecting us. Other concerns did knock around in my mind after Haider told me about Shabaz and the Balandi women. Would my designs on paper translate to the women? Would I even connect with them enough to partner with them? Was their work like the ones I'd seen in Global? I was still waiting for a reply to the email I'd sent to Shabaz promptly after getting home from Heat that would satisfy a few of my questions.

I told Haider I could have made a long list of what-ifs and he asked, "What are what-ifs?"

"They're like, if things don't work out. What if our car breaks down? What if I can't communicate with the women?"

"Do you have a list to counteract the what-ifs?"

"Not a list but I've imagined a successful Nisa for most of my life."

"What does that look like for you? Why not focus on that?" He stuck his hands in his pockets and his eyes fought the strands of my hair blowing across my face.

"You can do that so well. You don't know what I'm talking about but when we were kids you taught me something that's going to sound so cheesy now." I laughed at myself.

"You taught me to focus on just making contact with the cricket ball. Not how far or where the ball went, just to make contact. Things have worked out for me every time I've been able to think like that. I've always wanted to have a chance to tell you that."

"I don't remember that but you didn't answer my question: What does everything working out look like for you?"

I stopped walking, stuck my toes in the wet sand, "It looks like . . . the Balandi women are eager to show me their work, um, they can produce the jewelry. I know it sounds hasty but I can make a deal with them and I'll save their tradition and maybe even myself."

My truest hope for coming to Pakistan escaped like a breath held too long underwater. He stared at me and this time, I didn't shy away. We continued walking, cooling our feet in the foam left behind by the waves. "When you say *make a deal* you mean financially, right? Are you aware of how big that investment could be?"

"I told you, I came here for this. I have a general idea of the costs of starting a business here. My baba and I discussed it briefly before I left when this was not a reality yet and so, yes, I'm financially prepared. That's if things work out."

"Again, what-ifs? By the way, has Shabaz emailed you yet?"

Like dusting off something precious accidentally thrown away, I pressed repeatedly to open Shabaz's email sitting in my spam folder. I clicked the attached images before reading his introduction in the email. Haider turned to face me, blocking the sun so I could see my screen without the blinding glare. There were multiple pictures of metal beads, coins, links, and the Balandi women in rusty-red *shalwar kameezes* hunched over, in another picture sewing them together to construct an elaborate necklace. A blacksmith's hands were poised to pour liquid metal into molds and dozens of handmade disc-like coins waiting to be assembled. Ideas for Nisa rushed into my mind, dizzying me, and I plopped down in the sand to steady myself.

"You, ok?" Haider hunched down beside me. When I didn't answer he leaned in to peek at my phone.

"Haider, I want this. Exactly this. I'm going to start Nisa with the Balandi women."

"*Inshallah*, Hena." I repeated the same and put my phone away. I'd savor each picture again and reread the detailed email by Shabaz in the privacy of Dadi Jaan's room, where my tears of elation could free-fall.

Haider pointed his finger between me and a tasseled camel riding in our direction. My heart was still fluttering from the email when he jaunted his way up to the camel driver, expertly grabbed the reins and brought the impressive creature back to me. The camel lowered his head when Haider pulled on the reins. I petted its rough golden fur behind the ears the way you do a dog.

After some maneuvering, I was on the animal, holding tight and squealing so it scared the birds pattering in the sand to take flight. Haider didn't get on with me and gave the driver a couple extra rupees to let him take the camel for a short walk alone with me. The driver didn't hesitate, seeing how easily Haider handled the docile giant.

We turned around after doing a long lap on the quiet beach which was interrupted by my phone. Each time, Haider searched my face for an expression. I ignored every alert, letting him know I was entirely there with him and Musa was nonexistent. We made small talk about the weather in Quetta, what to pack, including my passport, how much money to take for spending, how we would drive for 11 hours starting in the morning with quick stops for food and bathroom breaks, and finally agreed we'd leave in two days when Skinner could best cover the classes at the music shop by himself.

The camel driver's face relaxed seeing me in one piece and his camel returned to him. A layer of orange evening light was settling over the ocean when Haider asked if I wanted to go home. His eyes smiled when I said no. When my phone rang, I flashed Baba's mustached contact picture that was lighting up the screen at Haider, signaling I had to answer.

"*Salaam alaikum*, is everything ok, Baba?"

"Yes, Hena *beti*. Everything is ok. Your chacha messaged me earlier and woke me up. I couldn't go back to sleep after. He says you're wanting to go on a trip into Balochistan?"

Haider could overhear the conversation and walked off to sit on a rocky mound near the alcove where we started.

"Quetta, Baba," I inserted, knowing the major city was more likely to win Baba's approval than the entire province of Balochistan or the unknown village I actually planned to visit. "I've been reading up on it and they've made these great highways for tourism. There's beautiful scenery and great food. Why have we never gone there before?" I tried to play on his guilt for never taking Omar and me on normal vacations instead of visiting family in the same city year after year.

"You live in California, what could be better?"

"Come on, Baba. You've told me about how beautiful those parts of Pakistan are as well."

"I know it is but I'm not sure it's safe for you."

"Baba. I wouldn't be going alone. Did Chacha tell you about that? I would be with Haider and Annie, Ghelani saab's kids. They're adults now, and we'd have a proper tour guide too."

"I don't know, *beti*."

"Baba, you know it's been a really hard year for me. I didn't get anywhere with the jeweler friends you suggested either. I'm hoping something will inspire me on this trip or at the least I will see another part of Pakistan. Dadi Jaan always wanted me to come and see more of it. We'll only be gone for two days at most. I really need this, Baba."

"Send me the information for the tour guide's company and I'll check them out and does Chacha know these other people you plan to go with?"

"Yeah, Baba. They've been neighbors for 30 years if not longer. You knew their dad too."

"Well, then have them come and talk to Chacha and . . ."

"I don't think we should impose anything else on Chacha. He has a lot going on."

"With what, you mean with the new tenants moving in?"

"I don't think they wanted anyone to move in in the first place and he wants to tell you something family related. He said he'd tell you himself."

Baba paused to let out a sigh. "I think I know what it is. Send me the tour guide information at least. Stay safe, I'll talk to you later."

Haider was shoving our unused tissues into the greasy burger bags. "If Annie were here, she'd want to keep those tissues."

"You noticed that about her too? I keep telling her to stop."

We both missed Annie. She exuded a gregarious energy when she wasn't raging at Haider. Still, it was the kind of energy that eluded us both. A thickening fog was drowning the residual daylight and a cold mist was chilling my arms. Haider threw our trash in the back seat and proceeded to slide a flyer for a tour guide company into my bag.

"It doesn't have to be a pretense for your dad, you could actually hire this tour guide to show you around."

"No, thanks. I'm satisfied with the guide I've got" I waited for him to open my door but he slid my bag down my arm and placed it in the car. "Stay outside with me for a bit." His lips parting gently at the beginning to every word. He searched my face with his eyes that glowed auburn in the depleting sunlight. Radiating warmth from his body diluted the cold breeze flowing around us. Tenderly, he pressed his warm lips against mine.

I sent Baba the tour guide companies information on my walk down Mausumbe Road where Haider let me out. Back home, Khalil surprised Chacha and Shenachi for dinner that evening. I hadn't seen him since my last visit and, then, only passing him in the hallway or at dinner if he didn't insist on eating in his room with a textbook on his lap. He'd gotten lankier but his face hadn't aged, holding onto his fuller cheeks, no facial hair and nerdy as ever. He barely made eye contact with me while we made small talk in the living room like guests. His voice only went up an octave when he spoke about work. Saadia who stayed late helping Shenachi in the kitchen announced that dinner was ready and rushed off to catch Surghum so he could give her a ride home, since it was too dark for her to walk.

Shenachi still babied Khalil, taking his food out for him and not troubling him to reach for the handmade *rotis*. Shenachi's face glowed, "*Mashallah*, my boy has a good appetite."

"Or Mom's food is just so delicious?" Chacha tried to engage Khalil in conversation, to which he barely looked up to pay a half smile, returning to his food. That's just how I remembered him. Hunched over books, not allowed to play outside on even mildly hot days, brought home early from family events because he had an exam the next day or sneezed twice in a row. Chacha and Dadi Jaan would argue that he needed to be more social but Shenachi's maternal instincts, however distorted, always reigned. No one could argue with her either since she'd start crying uncontrollably, lamenting her other two boys that died only weeks before birth. With the loss she'd suffered, she'd earned the right to over-mother.

"I spoke to your baba again. He said you sent him information on the touring company and it looks good. I'd like to see it too."

"What touring company is it?" Khalil suddenly spoke.

"Caravan Pakistan."

With a piece of *roti* sticking to his lip he confirmed, "I know that company. They are the official tourism company for all of Sindh. I went to the tourism center about six and quarter months ago to pick up a flyer for an American colleague of mine. I had a terribly hard time finding the travel brochures they offered. They haven't placed them in a visible location for optimal exposure. If they place them askew a bit next to the clerk's station, it would be best."

While Shenachi swooned over her son's fluency in English, Chacha's eyebrows furrowed at the obvious strangeness of his conjecture. "Well? What did your friend think of the company and did he have a safe trip?"

"He said their service was exceptional but quite expensive and since he made it back to work on Monday, I imagine it was safe." Corners of his face pulled up into a strange smile on his attempt at humor. Overly enthused, Shenachi laughed loudly and Chacha showed a sincere smile.

"So, will it be a private tour for you and your friends or with a group of tourists?" Chacha's inquiries weren't ending.

"There will be a small group plus my friend and her brother."

"You know, I didn't even know Ghelani Saab had a daughter until you told me," Shenachi inserted and nudged her son's elbow at the mention of a single girl. "They do the yoga together, *chuthth pey*," signaling to the rooftop with her greasy finger.

"Yoga. Most beneficial to the . . ." I drifted as he started on his encyclopedic facts on yoga. Chacha interrupted him to tell Shenachi about a plumbing issue upstairs and that the tenants would be moving in in two days, later than originally expected. *Just in time to provide a distraction for my departure*, I thought.

After helping Shenachi clear the table, I declined their invitation for chai but Shenachi called me back, "Be careful on your trip. Ghelani saab's Haider from what I know of him is a decent man but he is a man and that girl, well, Surghum says she's a strange one. I haven't spoken to Bushra about her yet. She would know more."

"Shenachi, Bushra Auntie thinks badly about everyone but trust me I'll be careful. Now, go, go, spend some time with Khalil before he has to head back. I'll wash the dishes."

She looked longingly into the dining room at the sound of her son's laughter, wiped her hands on a dishrag to join them and ordered, "Leave the dishes for Saadia to do in the morning, she hardly does anything around here anyway."

I could hear the murmurs of their conversation on the porch while I replied to texts from Musa and Annie and ignored Omar's, Mom's and Kristen's messages, saving my reply to Shabaz for last. To Musa, I sent an apology with the excuse of having a family obligation and asked him to look me up when he visited LA in the fall.

I promised I would take him to the beach "sans the camels though." He wrote back, *It's a date!* Annie's text, however, was asking me to check my email for some list. I was curious but wanted a moment to relive the warmth of Haider's kiss in my mind. Unconsciously, I was touching my lips when Ameer's face flashed in my mind. Guilt shot through the satisfying moment. Ameer felt like another lifetime, somewhere in the past but accessible in the moment through a pained memory. How could I enjoy the pleasure of the evolving chemistry between Haider and me without closure with Ameer, and wasn't this all too soon and going too fast?

Annie's text, *did you get my email?* averted my attention. The email she had pestered me about was also in my spam folder with an unrecognizable email address, far too many numbers and underscores. In it was an itinerary for our trip entitled *Nisa's Adventure* and another email with a neat spreadsheet of expenses. Haider must have convinced her quickly, like he said he would. The expense sheet was concise, with a van rental and a two-night hotel stay which I would pay for. Under food and gas was H/A for Haider and Annie, something the two of them would take care of, and under tour guide fee was a heart emoji. I called Annie right away.

"I'm so excited!"

"Me too! I'm so glad you agreed to go."

We giddily spoke for an hour. I gushed about the pictures Shabaz had sent and how I knew this was going to be the start of Nisa. She told me to hire her full time as her assistant when the business took off so she could quit her job at the tutoring center and break her lovesick student's heart. Haider's voice in the background pulled me to our kiss. "Tell her not to take too much cash, she can always withdraw more from any bank in Quetta, if needed."

I hung up to say goodbye to Khalil, who was leaving with towering containers of food, when Haider texted for me to help him pick something out for Annie's birthday; he specified *something practical*. Annie and I had already made plans tomorrow afternoon to go shopping for a couple of warm things to wear in the chilly region, leaving the day before the trip for me to pack and collect all of my notes and questions for the Balandi women. Haider and I would be left with the evening to secretly shop for Annie.

Baba sent multiple messages telling me to be careful on the trip and a few for me to enjoy myself. My replies consisted of the stellar reviews of the tour guide company and, of course, the seal of approval from Khalil to assure him.

Eleven

I treated Annie to lunch at a quiet restaurant after we both bought cheaply made fur-lined boots. While we waited for our food, I felt there was something she wanted to say but struggled. I caught her repeatedly staring at me. At my notice, she'd look down at the colored-glass vase with the silk flowers on our table or at the painting of a schooner behind me.

"Is something wrong, Annie?"

"Hena. Please don't hate me for asking but do you have feelings for Haider? I guess I know you do but how strong are your feelings?" Her eyes frowned with concern. After the warning Haider gave me about Annie's protective quills activating, I couldn't divulge my true feelings of how he wasn't just a crush, instead a constant shadow following me since childhood; elusive, not tangible until now.

Soothingly I spoke, "Annie, I think he's cute, that's it, and you know I just got out of a relationship, an entire engagement. I'm happy I've made friends with both of you and I couldn't ask for more than that." Her small smile told me she was satisfied. Just in time, sizzling skewers of meat on reflective silver plates were placed between us.

"Shabaz and I have been emailing back and forth since yesterday and he told me about this woman they call Mai that we'll be meeting. She's the head artisan, she teaches the younger women how to do the work, the traditional way. A part of me wishes I could tell my dad about it and wish he could go with me too."

"Go check it out for yourself first. You're an independent woman and, you know, you've come this far on your own."

"You're right and thanks, Annie."

"For what?"

"For believing in me. It would be amazing if I made the deal with Mai on my own."

"You mentioned your dad has a business too. I'm sure it runs in the family. What kind of business does he have?"

We talked for an hour about businesses in the US vs. Pakistan. I proudly relished telling her about Baba's achievements in the medical supply industry, the consistent growth of his company, and how much I wanted him to retire to travel with Mom. I explained I had no interest in taking the reins of the business from him—Omar would take on that burden. Annie listened like I was telling her a bedtime story, her eyes brightening when I told her about Baba's success and dimming when I spoke about his humble beginnings.

She didn't have to be at work for a few hours yet but I had to cut our day together short if I wanted to get to the bank before it closed.

Annie whined, "We still have more shopping to do, I haven't found the right jacket yet."

"I think I have something that might fit you, I'll send you pics tonight." Satisfied she wouldn't have to spend money on an item of clothing she'd never be able to use again, she agreed but asked, "What's your rush to get home today?"

"I volunteered to help Shenachi get the upstairs ready for the tenants and I have to stop off at the bank too for some spending cash." A compact iLift picked us up at the noisy intersection in front of the restaurant, making a stop near the cathedral to let Annie off. "Don't forget to pack the jacket for me, I hope it'll do or I'll be a popsicle in Quetta!" She said, chattering her teeth.

Fast slapping sounds of my flip-flops on the driveway made Surghum pull his head out of the hood of the car.

"Surghum, I need to go to the bank." Clearly offended again at me taking an iLift home instead of calling him to pick me up, he muttered something under his breath. Slowly he extracted the dipstick and began to inspect the motor oil frustratingly slowly like he was trying to read his name on a grain of rice. "It's not safe to take an iLift to the bank, you told me that, remember? Plus, their drivers can't get you anywhere on time. The bank is closing in 30 minutes. I need to get there right away." I appealed to his innate need to get his passengers to their destinations on time.

"Just let me wash my hands, you get in Hena bibi."

A man dressed in a navy-blue suit and a striped red tie who reminded me of every male flight attendant I'd ever seen asked me to take a seat and offered a customary cup of chai that I politely declined. Upon his desk was a Pakistani green Onyx pen holder with a gold name plate: Fareed Rahman, Murad Bank.

Doubtful the Murad Bank account Dadi Jaan had lovingly set up for me had enough funds to take me to Quetta, I inquired about withdrawing from my American bank account.

"How much would you like to withdraw?" I knew if I wanted a large amount, I'd have to have my bank back home safely clear it and that could take a few days.

I still had most of the $1,500 of spending cash I'd brought with me that Chacha exchanged for rupees but having the kind of money that would possibly be needed for any major transactions for Nisa in hand meant I was entirely prepared. Not being able to access it right away felt like a shortcoming, hinting at a lack of commitment.

My hands slumped onto my empty bag, and as a final inquiry, I asked Fareed to give me the balance in my Murad account. He struck his manicured fingers on his keyboard and slid a balance receipt across the desk. The string of numbers didn't compute in my head. 1,224,125.00 rupees.

When I reached for my phone to calculate it in dollars, he struck his keys again, "You want to know what that is in dollars, right?"

"Yes, please."

"That's nearly $7,000 US."

"No, excuses." I whispered to myself.

"Pardon?"

"I'd like to make a withdrawal."

Behind the steel door of the bank's bathroom stall, I unzipped the secret compartment under my bag that housed a lonely passport and squeezed the large stacks of money deep into it. Feeling the heaviness of my bag on my shoulder anchored me to my commitment to start Nisa with the Balandi women. Finally, I said a quiet *thank you* to Dadi Jaan.

Back at home, I stuck my bag into the zippered section of my suitcase and pushed it under the bed. Shenachi knocked at my door for dinner and I responded quickly, "Shenachi, I'm not hungry at all, eat without me please."

A few moments later, sounds of a political-debate show blared from the living room where Chacha and Shenachi were eating their dinner. Afterwards, they had their chai and watched a game show, with Shenachi repeatedly yelling out answers and Chacha disagreeing. When Dadi Jaan was alive, we always had dinner in the dining room; their routine had clearly changed. Having dinner in the dining room the way we did when Dadi Jaan was alive must have just been for me.

Seeing Haider bite his calloused thumb, helpless in a women's boutique, made me laugh to myself. When he saw me approaching, his face relaxed and he pointed to a red purse with far too many compartments.

"Annie would use that. It's cute how well you know your sister." I could see her wearing it across her body with the Swiss flag dress. Just so my being there wouldn't appear totally useless, I thumbed through a rack of blouses and he followed behind me, his arms folded against a band tee-shirt whose name was half readable under his black vest. Me in my black peasant dress, hair wild after losing my last hair tie somewhere in Surghum's car made us look like the cover of a vintage Fleetwood Mac record. We looked entirely out of place in this city. Yet, we seamlessly matched each other.

At the sounds of the nearby stores shutting their doors earlier than we expected, I urged, "I think you should get that purse, think it's really her." We had both been running late to meet today. He was stuck at work and I was busy meticulously highlighting important notes in a Nisa booklet I'd put together for Shabaz and this Mai, who I couldn't wait to meet. In it were design ideas, sketches of simple and a few intricate jewelry pieces, a small list of questions I had, and lastly, interview questions for the Balandi women that I could later use to create a story for Nisa's marketing campaign. Thanks to Annie, my design ideas were bound together neatly, free of charge from the tutoring center which she disguised as a project for one of her students.

We meandered slowly through racks of clothing, choosing our own paths to the counter to pay. A tall security guard waited to lock the front door and stared us down to move along. We didn't have the time alone we both secretly hoped for, like we did on the beach the other day.

Haider opened his wallet and a blurry picture of him on his ID flashed. Haider with a fuzzy beard was almost unrecognizable. I recollected that my driver's license picture didn't pay me any compliments either. I teased him to let me see the picture and knocked the wallet out of his hands. Its leather made a slap on the floor and the guard at the door huffed with annoyance. Haider picked it up and slid it deep into the front pocket of his fitted jeans, unintentionally tucking a corner of his tee-shirt in with it. It pulled his shirt down, stretching two cigarette holes on the neckline that resembled the piercing of a vampire's fangs. The sales girl slowly counted the money, looking at us in between each swipe of the colorful bills.

"I need to grab my guitar from Skinner's apartment; it'll only take a minute. I would hate to miss a chance to hear what my guitar sounds like in the open air. The acoustics in the mountains should be awesome."

"He lives at the music shop."

"Not at, but above it."

I was curious to see Skinner's apartment if only to report back to Annie, though she'd never confided she had a thing for him. When we arrived, he reached for my seat belt, and I lifted my arms to allow him to satisfy his impulse.

Haider walked through the music class walls to a rusty metal staircase and then out of sight. The class was being set up by a boy that could have been Skinner's little brother or even his son. *Tablas* were placed on velveted donut-shaped rings and a big circular drum with a leathered tip mallet was at the forefront of the class. I tapped my finger on the drum and made a flat sound. The boy told me to pick it up and try again. I struck my middle finger against it and made a deep thump that vibrated my arm, the sound resonating in the air for a while before disappearing.

Haider appeared from the top of the stairs. Securing his phone between his head and his shoulder, he gestured for me to come up with a scoop of his hand. When cymbals crashed to the floor downstairs, he pressed his hand against his ear to hear Skinner on the phone. He disappeared behind a barricade of boxes that separated a small eating area fit with a single chair and a yellow table that reflected a metal filing cabinet next to a modest-size bed on its epoxied surface.

"Fucking Skinner, he has three Fenders and had to take mine," he whined. "He says he'll bring it to my house by morning but the guy has never woken up before noon in his life. I can drop you off and come back to get it tonight." Dripping sounds of *tablas* being struck and the chatter of students in the background signaled class had started.

"Don't worry about me. I'll just call an iLift to pick me up." My voice competed with the music penetrating the room.

When I tapped my phone on to dial for the ride, Haider held his hands close to his mouth in a cone shape trying to magnify his voice. "Don't do that." The drumming downstairs stopped. "You came out just to help me, I can at least drive you home. Skinner said he'll be here with my guitar in an hour or so. If you don't mind waiting."

He pulled up two wooden crates for us to sit on, respectfully avoiding Skinner's bed next to us. Trickling sounds of *tablas* started once again following the stentorian voice of a teacher who instructed *ta ta ta*.

"Do you play any instruments?"

"I played clarinet in my high school's symphonic band. My brother played it before me so it was handed down to me. I would've never chosen it. It makes a terrible goose-like sound. My dad wanted me to play the flute because he said it sounded '*svvwweet*.'"

"And what did you want to play?" He asked, pointing his finger towards me.

"The drums actually."

"Why drums?"

"They were loud . . . awake." I explained.

"I have a friend who says we're drawn to the instruments that can speak for us. Whatever we can't say, we try to through music."

"It's funny you say that because I used to love the sound of thunder, something about the booming was so loud and clear. I guess I felt unheard back then, as all girls tend to in their teens."

"And do you still like the drums?"

"I guess, I do. The *tablas* are kinda' speaking to me right now. What does 'ta, ta' mean? I've always heard them explained with those sounds"

"Here, let me see your hand."

He held it face up on his knee. With his rough fingertip he drew a circle on my palm followed by a smaller one inside. "The center is the *siahi* and this is the *maidan*." He explained the parts of the *tabla* and how certain words corresponded with where the circles were struck, making very specific sounds. He transported me back again to our childhood where I nervously held a cricket bat in my clammy hands, when he wasn't looking at me but rather to the soul within that was capable of learning anything it was taught. Only this time, he paused between his tutelage to feel the softness of my palms, transgressing beyond the circles of the *siahi* and *maidan*. He tapped twice then recited, 'ta . . . ta . . .' then tapped the center of the *siahi*, 'din' with a concluding sound making the instrument speak where we could not.

Slowly, his tapping faded on my palm when the *tablas* grew louder, rising in tempo and rattling the string of clarinets and reed flutes overhead. We kissed in rhythm to the music until we rose up from the crates and he pressed me against the cool bricks of the wall. Air whistled in through a crack in the window with the whispering scent of cardamom and charcoal from a pot of chai brewing downstairs and tandoori lamb sizzling over a flame in some nearby restaurant. I slid my hands into his vest and he slid his up my dress. Music filled the room, the way it filled our bodies.

THE RENTERS' ARRIVAL THAT NIGHT, instead of the next morning, came as a surprise to the whole house. Shenachi shouted commands at Surghum to park the car on the street so the driveway would be free for the renters to unload their furniture. Surghum insisted that there would be enough room for both vehicles, not letting on that he didn't want dirt from the street being kicked up onto the recently washed car. Chacha was all about pleasantries and kept asking the family if they wanted to come in and have some chai before starting the laborious work of unloading the contents of their lives to the second floor. The middle-aged father walked away backwards, thanking Chacha profusely, and suggested chai for another day. The box of toiletries he was carrying nearly slipped out of his hands when he turned the corner to the stairs, scrunching a plastic bag that showed the curved neck of a green *lota*. His little girl followed behind with a small folded blanket tucked under her arm.

No one but the family's little boy, who was rolling an over-stuffed suitcase, noticed when I slipped in through the side gate and entered Dadi Jaan's room through the porch. The wheels of the boy's suitcase stopped rolling for a moment to make sense of my dark figure moving about. He went on once his mom called for him to hurry up.

Pensive thoughts about him entered my mind. This boy was to start his life in a new home, a new school, away from his friends with only his sister as a playmate. At first, they'd stick close together watching the other kids play in the neighborhood. Then, one of them would get invited to join in and the other would have to watch on the sidelines until they'd made their own friends— just like the two friends I'd made here. I reflected in the shower, washing Haider's scent off my body.

Twelve

Saadia was taking a generous breakfast to the family upstairs on Chacha's request. Punctual Surghum paced the driveway and I quietly told Saadia to get Surghum a second cup of chai while he waited for me to get ready. Once he finished, he started his pacing again, peering into the house and periodically announcing the time.

Shenachi shooed him, suggesting he practice discretion since we weren't the only people living in the house now; a sharp-eared young family had moved in upstairs and the happenings of our household shouldn't be announced to them. Annie messaged me to head out and I grabbed my heavy duffle bag, double checked my handbag for my wallet, sketch tablet, Nisa booklets, and felt for the stacks of cash and passport in the bottom.

With Chacha already at work, Shenachi walked me to the car and instructed, "Cover up when you're there. People aren't as modern in those areas as here and you don't want to attract any attention." If I closed my eyes, it could have been Mom talking.

As we drove off, Surghum asked if I'd met the family who'd moved in last night. He didn't wait for my response and started on about Shenachi and Chacha not knowing how to keep tenants in their place. He scoffed at them being given the parking spot nearest the gate which meant he'd have to ask them to back their car out each time he needed to be let out.

"Soon, they will be asking to borrow this or that, take me here or there real quick and I'm not their driver too." But soon his eyed softened and he admitted their children's laughter would bring life into the quiet house, "Like with your Thia Kuli's kids or when you and Omar used to visit. I used to give Omar piggyback rides around the house until my shoulders ached." He laughed at a distant memory.

When we arrived, Annie peeked out of the touring company's lobby door and waved me in. Surghum waggled his head, impressed with the small group of white tourists boarding a spotless bus with the words *Caravan Pakistan - Fully Air Conditioned* printed on its side. "Hena bibi please keep us updated through your trip and call if you have any trouble."

We boarded our rental van, parked around the corner, from the visitor center after Surghum drove off. When Haider and I made eye contact, an uncontrollable smile erupted on my face. He bent over to load my duffle bag into the back of the van, reached for my leather bag to join the rest of the luggage but I pulled it away. "I'll keep this up front with me."

"Sure. And Hena, let's try to be discreet."

"And, good morning, how are you?" I said without expression, getting into the van. He rushed around "Sorry. I'm great, really great. How are you?" He rubbed his stubble to hide a smile that was slowly parting his lips.

Annie, who called shotgun, tapped on her window at us, "Let's go, let's go!"

I saw her reflection in the sideview mirror, her eyes trying to read my face. Haider checked Annie's seat belt latch before starting the car and she rolled her eyes. Once we got onto the Lyari Expressway, Annie began fiddling with the music to finally stop at the piercing sound of some Bollywood song.

"Garbage music."

"Too bad. We had a deal."

Grabbing the headrest of her seat, Annie turned herself all the way around to face me. Her big round eyes searched for something to talk about.

"Why don't we play a game? Like Antakshari."

I gave her a thumbs-down and Haider too vetoed her idea.

"You guys are boring. We have like over 11 hours to kill, you know." She pouted. "At least, let's ask each other those get-to-know questions."

Sleep was looming in both Haider's and my eyes but I agreed to entertain Annie in hopes of tiring her out like Omar and Ayesha did with baby Zain. An hour into the open stretch of the National Highway, Annie began running out of the usual what's your favorite color, food, place to visit, etc., to which Haider and I both answered robotically.

"Ok, ok, I got a good one, what's your biggest fear? Hena, you go first."

I leaned in between their seats and drew in a deep breath which brought in Haider's familiar scent. It took me a while to shuffle through my many fears to answer: fear of disappointing my parents, fear of getting fat, fear of Ameer hating me forever, but I chose to tell them about my reoccurring dream of falling.

"But what does 'falling' mean?" Annie craned her neck to ask.

"Well, teeth falling out is supposed to be a vanity dream but the actual falling . . . to me it means losing control or losing my chance to prove myself." I answered. Simultaneously, Annie shot

Haider a glance and he pressed his lips together. With so many of my hopes riding on this trip, had they felt the pressure of ensuring it was successful?

"No matter the outcome of this trip, whether things work out or not, I'm grateful for both of your help. I know it'll be a transformative experience. It kinda' already is."

Forgetting to be discreet about his feelings, Haider blurted out, "It's been quite an experience for me too."

"What about you, Annie?"

"Oh, that's easy. My fear is being alone."

Abandonment issues, I decided and began drawing immediate connections. The overly friendly personality and jealousy over seeing her brother's attention be distributed must have meant she was afraid she'd be left behind. Poor Annie, all alone. Where I should have felt compassion, I felt an annoyance over her childish hang-ups. Annie poked Haider's arm with her sharp finger to go next but suddenly changed her mind, suggesting as we were all friends we could ask more personal questions. Haider shook his head side to side at Annie but she continued.

"Hena, you told me about your breakup with your fiancé, sorry ex-fiancé, but I still don't understand the exact reason for the breakup. Was there like unfaithfulness or something?"

If it wasn't for the smug look on her face, the question wouldn't have been entirely off limits. I intended to answer fully with details just to shame her for picking on my guilt-filled wound, a wound she must have known was just beginning to heal, when the deafening sound of Haider slamming his hand on the dash prevented me.

"Why the fuck would you ask that question?"

"Hena and I are friends and I can ask her things like that, right, Hena?" Her eyes darted, waiting for my answer.

"No more questions, Annie. I intend to fill the next couple of hours sleeping. Haider, wake me when you get tired and I can drive." I lay myself across the back seat using my bag as a lumpy pillow. Annie nervously searched her bag and came up with a snack to share, an ill-timed peace offering. I placed my arm over my eyes, ignoring her. She pushed the bag towards Haider, and he too rejected it, withdrawing from her into the window to bite the callouses on his fingers.

In the quiet humming of the car, sleep should have come easy. Instead, I spent three hours awake with competing thoughts of Annie's hurtful question and images of Haider and I last night. Two disparate feelings; one of guilt and resentment and the other of release and pleasure, just like the sweet pain of a sore muscle being massaged.

Finally, Annie broke the silence in the car by unsuccessfully muffling the sound of the crinkling bag she'd offered earlier. An undeniable sulfur stench filled the van. When I uncovered my eyes to determine its source, I saw that it was the same savory chickpea snack Mom had been banned from eating around the rest of the family. Haider grabbed the bag from Annie's hands and violently tossed it out of the window.

"I told you not to bring that with you!" he roared from his gut. Annie's eyes filled with shock, her hands frozen as if she were still holding the bag. I sat up when Haider swerved off the road and the wheels of the van screeched to a stop. A cloud of dust wrapped itself around us. When the van door slammed, Haider had left. Wind began to sweep the dust away. I could see the crease in Haider's back, exposed by his shirt whipping up and around his body. He fought strong gusts to make his way towards a roadside restaurant.

I put my hand on Annie's headrest, attempting to let her know I hadn't left her too but she pulled away like she always did. It was enough, I was done consoling her. Sliding open the van door, I jumped out, trying to catch up to Haider with the new weight in my bag slowing me down. My voice calling out to him was lost in the blustering winds. When he slowed, I made it a few steps past him and walked backwards facing him, not letting him pull away.

Trying to catch my breath, I shouted, "What's wrong with you two? This is insane! I can't handle this, Haider." I finally broke down. The weight of the lies I had told Baba about this trip, the surge of unexpected pleasure I experienced with Haider, guilt over getting involved with a man so quickly after Ameer, Annie's bipolar behavior that left me feeling uncertain from moment to moment, and most of all, my dream of Nisa coming to fruition, a mere eight hours away, surged from my eyes in the form of tears, tears that the winds rerouted to my temples.

The vein in Haider's forehead pumped slower seeing my frustration. Leading me by the hand, he pulled me out of Annie's sight and to the blinding whitewashed walls of the side of the lone *kebab* and naan restaurant. The chipped edges of the sand-blasted wall, exposing the bricks underneath, blocked the harsh wind enough for me to tame my hair around my face. Haider ran his hands through his hair, puffed up his cheeks, and let out an exhausted sigh. He stood against a faded mural of a devilish red bull with a nose ring, its horns precisely framing Haider's head.

"I'm overwhelmed. A few weeks ago, I fled, actually fled from my home to be here alone. For what? To chase a stupid dream with a crazy emotional girl and her angry brother? You're throwing her snacks out of the window? What next, you're going to throw her out of the running car before we get to Quetta? I'm so close and so far away, it's killing me inside."

Putting his arm around my shoulder, he spoke softly into the side of my face, "I know you're disappointed that you're stuck with us on this trip. There's a lot you don't know about our lives, but Hena, it's not Annie or me that's overwhelming you. If not our fighting, something else would upset you. I know this is all out of your realm. You're Pakistani but American mostly. Roadblocks and struggles are not a part of your everyday life. If you wanted a smooth ride, then maybe Musa would have been a better choice. Hena, I'm just not him."

I peeled his heavy arm away, nearly dropping my bag, and debated if I should walk away from him forever, for being reduced to first world problems. But hearing him admit that he could not size up to the privileged Musas and Henas of the world softened my indignation.

"Haider, there's a lot about me you don't know either. I know one thing about you though. It's that you couldn't survive a day in the life of any woman, a privileged one like me or a struggling, screwed up one like Annie." I rubbed the tears from my wet face and Haider suddenly pulled me into a forceful hug. My face buried in the cocoon of his chest where I wished I could have stayed but broke away to demand, "You have to tell me why you and Annie fight like this; it's strange and it can't be over her choice of snacks. I feel completely in the dark. I'm not continuing on this trip unless you explain."

At the sound of Annie's whimpering from around the corner, Haider spoke quickly, "I'll tell you once we're on the road. Switch seats with Annie. I'll explain. I promise. I'm going to get us something to eat since we're here." Fighting his way through the winds again, he shouted at us to get back in the van. Sobbing, Annie appeared gripping the sides of a wall to anchor herself from blowing away.

"I know I'm ruining the trip. I'm so sorry. I know you must hate me but I care about you a lot, way more than Haider, you know. I started getting a migraine last night and it's just getting worse. It's making things worse for everyone."

Her eyes were bloodshot and swollen. Drying winds and the huge tears that splashed her cheeks made them look worse. I accepted her remorse but resigned her to the backseat for the rest of the trip.

Back on the road, when Annie's snoring became too loud, Haider and I took turns listening to each other's music. I introduced him to the California band Young the Giant, and he educated me on why Don Felder was kicked out of the Eagles. I handed him a morsel of *kebab* wrapped in cold naan that he dropped trying to avoid hitting a slow-moving goat on the highway while the herder whistled for it to come to him. I insisted he keep both hands on the wheel and fed him a piece by hand with my finger grazing his lips.

"So, it's time to explain."

He looked back at a sleeping Annie. "Fear, like her question earlier. My fear is death."

"Fear of dying?"

"Well, not my death but my loved ones and the fear that I won't be able to save them."

"Did you always have this fear?" I coaxed him to elaborate, the way you do when you lure a timid animal to you.

"Annie and I were in a car accident; my dad was too." He paused to let out a long steady sigh. "He died on the way to the hospital. Doctors said it wasn't from injuries. Apparently, he had a heart attack. Annie was hospitalized with head trauma and laceration to the abdomen. Those migraines she has are a lingering side effect. That's when she picked up yoga. She says it helps. Anyway, she was hurt the most since she was on the side that was hit."

"The laceration. That's the scar on Annie's hip . . ."

"Yeah, she was holding this dish of dessert on her lap that she'd made to take to my dad's friend's house for dinner. The dish broke on impact and a piece stabbed her like a knife. Hena, I walked away untouched."

"Is that why you buckle people in or do that seat belt latch check?"

"Bingo. Is that the correct American word?"

I gave him a nod and closed my eyes for a moment to acknowledge that he knew about loss in a way I could only imagine.

"I'm so sorry, that must have been so painful for you and your family."

"That's another American thing." He said pointing a finger up. "Saying sorry. You didn't cause the accident, so why sorry?"

"I mean, I'm sorry to hear."

He placed his hand on his chest where I had the other night, "Anyway, Annie and I stuck to each other after the accident even more. We're all each other has."

"And your mom."

"Yeah. Right, of course. Still, we're on our own; working and supporting everything ourselves. Lately, Annie and I have started drifting apart, it's bound to happen but it really scares her."

"What about for you?"

He turned up the faint music coming out of the speakers. It signaled he'd done enough sharing. At the risk of sounding uncompassionate or too sheltered to understand, the way he had basically deemed me back at our detour, I didn't want to keep pressing. His explanation would have to suffice for now.

Annie woke up to eat when we stopped to use the bathroom and fell back asleep. I too dozed on and off, occasionally asking Haider to let me drive so he could rest. Though after hearing of his tragedy on the road, I doubted he'd even blink for more than a second or let me drive on the opposite side of the road for the first time. At our last pit stop for gas, he stopped me short of offering to get behind the wheel again, by shushing me and telling me to go back to sleep.

Chill filled the van that made me reach for my cardigan. It still smelled like cigarettes and hookah smoke from Heat. Black mountains in the dark sky began to appear. We had long entered the city of Quetta but needed to travel through it to reach our hotel that was situated high above the city, deep in the mountains. When I rolled the window down to take in a crisp breath of mountain air, Annie woke. A long indention on her cheek from the seam on the backseat that pressed against her face resembled the wretched scar on her abdomen.

THE SWEETHEART HOTEL, read a heavy carved wooden plaque across the front of the hotel, which was nestled in the side of mountainous terrain. Overlooking the twinkling Quetta valley below, we stretched while a boy dressed in a 1920's bellboy uniform unloaded our duffle bags and Annie's mini rolling suitcase. I held tight to the warm leather of my bag and took in a sip of icy air through my teeth.

"Which way is Balandi?" I exhaled the question.

"Around that steep mountain, still 40 minutes from here."

I made a rigid twist with my body to point myself in the direction we were to travel in the morning. A narrow dirt path, wide enough for only one vehicle, wound up to a dark rocky mountain and disappeared around the bend.

Annie checked us in at the marble counter of the lobby. An ornate fireplace sent sparks dangerously close to the bare feet of a guest who'd taken his shoes and socks off to dry. The woman he was with rested her head on a tufted wingchair, her head covered in a parka's hood with a shawl peeking through. I would have guessed they were a middle-aged couple on an anniversary getaway but the henna on her hands and an array of gold rings on her plump fingers more likely meant they were newlyweds on their honeymoon.

"You and I are in room four Hena, Haider, you're in five." Annie spoke as she dangled the keys to our room on her finger.

"Have you seen *The Shining*?" I asked Haider, who was staring at heavy floor to ceiling curtains.

"This is the Pakistani version." He smirked.

Annie and I giggled, making way for the bellboy to race up the pink carpeted staircase to get our bags to our rooms before us. We declined dinner with Haider at some restaurant he'd spotted in the city below which would mean getting back in the van again.

"I would rather walk there or starve." Annie squeezed her temples hard making her eyebrows zigzag and went straight into the bathroom. Haider and I lingered in our doorways; an unspoken invitation to his room floated in the hallway that neither of us could afford to accept with Annie around. I said goodnight and he blinked in acceptance.

Following Annie's itinerary, I set the alarm on my phone and called Chacha, telling him enthusiastically how quickly the time passed on the road and how beautiful the scenery was. I texted Baba pictures of the Balochistani desert from our drive and the lunch of *kebab* and empty bottles of Pakola with a *We're at the hotel, it's been a fun trip so far. Love you!*

I went through the room, committing the moment to memory to revisit later. Mindfully, I followed the swirls in the floral pattern on the walls, ran my finger across the dusty lampshade next to my head, felt the chill on my skin that came in through the crack in the balcony door. I listened to Annie's soft steps across the creaking floor as she tested out each chair in the room and looked in every drawer, pausing in between to massage her temples. She finally made her way to her bed where she began taking a concoction of medications, I was unaware she even needed. Before taking each pill, she mouthed *Bismillah*, her tiny throat expanding with each swallow like a sparrow taking sips from a puddle of water and coming up to look around before going for more.

Eventually, I surrendered the idea of sleep altogether and decided to have one more proud look at the Nisa booklets. Running my hand across the sketches, I panicked for a moment thinking I'd used the American system instead of metric to show the dimensions of my designs. Thoughts of having made some crucial mistake in explaining a design or business plan in simplified English kept me awake all night cross-referencing Shabaz's language in his emails to me, and then to the lingo in my booklet.

Powering off my laptop and letting my eyes adjust to the natural light that was filling the room, I walked to the balcony to confirm that dawn was peeking over the jagged mountaintops. It was a bit late for the morning prayer but I offered it still on the cold balcony. I poured my wishes into the palms of my hands—some for Nisa to work out the way I imagined and the day ahead to go smoothly; mostly, for my heart to always persevere. I'd made it this far and didn't want bumps in the road to stop me. Wiping my palms over my face at the end felt like sealing the prayer into my being.

Annie got dressed at her leisure, deciding against the jacket I had lent her and was all smiles about a reversible red puffer she'd found in the back of Haider's closet, a jacket he'd held onto since he was a preteen. The investment, worn once, didn't allow itself to be thrown away and eventually fit Annie's petite frame. To her, the 15 minutes she spent deciding on whether to wear the red or black side out was worth Haider's second knock on the door, urging us to come down.

"Stop, you don't smell," Annie scolded when she caught me sniffing the lapel of my tweed coat, which Shenachi had seemed eager to pawn off on me. When I remembered it was Dadi Jaan's, I couldn't refuse it. It was a coat she wore to my elementary school holiday performance of *The Nutcracker* the year she visited us in America. At the event, Dadi Jaan had taken off her gold chain with an ornate ruby pendant and placed it around my neck, insisting it was a festive color. But it had made me stand out amongst the other ballerinas and hit me in the face when I leapt across the stage. Backstage, it was a different story and all my friends had touched it like it was a good-luck charm. It had the Sugar Plum Fairy crying to her mom that she should've been the one wearing it, not a brown girl playing a mere snowflake fairy.

In the lobby, Haider was resting two cups of chai on the headrests of the wingchairs in an attempt to save us the seats. I picked up my tired pace and relieved him of one of the cups. Annie was still cascading down, testing Haider's patience.

Before another argument could erupt between them, I offered, "Let's just have our chai in the car. It'll save time." When I took the other cup from him so he could bring the van around, our hands touched but the sparks we shared the other night didn't ignite this time.

"Annie, we're running late. Let's move." I rushed. Annie sighed, shoving her hands in her pockets. I took quick gulps of my chai, hoping the burst of caffeine would energize me. Annie took her usual tiny sips. The cold stung our cheeks, and our breath visible in the air temporarily blinded the snowy mountains all around. Slushy snow crunched under my feet and it reminded me of how far I'd come. Haider checked Annie's seat belt and pulled down the visor on her side to shade her squinting eyes.

"Shabaz called twice already. He's been waiting for us for half an hour and it'll take another half an hour to get to him if we drive fast."

Annie, unfazed by Haider's complaining, pushed the visor up to look around at our sparkly surroundings. The piercing sun and snow made everything it hit twinkle. I looked down at the last drop of chai that rolled around in my cup, tipped the cup and gave it a tap with my finger to make it roll into my mouth.

"She didn't sleep all night," Annie told Haider, who shot my drowsy eyes a look in the rearview mirror.

"Get some sleep now. I'll wake you when we get close." With that he turned up a song that pleased Annie.

She yelped, "Nazia Hasan!"

"I put it on my playlist, thought you'd like it." The smile on his face widened to match hers. They went back and forth in conversation about the last time they were here and whether the restaurant where they ate, *Dum Pukht*, was still around. I went in and out of sleep, trying to get comfortable across the back seat that was warmed by the sunlight. Hearing Haider and Annie having a pleasant conversation for a change gave me assurance that they wouldn't kill each other if I dozed for a bit.

Nagging sounds of goats being herded across the road kept me conscious of reality but dreamlike visions entered my mind as if I was in a deep sleep. Snippets of Baba sitting in the tea parlor having his chai out of pink toy tea cups and then, of a lone Ameer hiking the trail I forced him to go once, lulled me.

My heavy eyelids parted to barely make out the blurry shadows of Haider and Annie over the center console, their foreheads touching. The strange image jarred me to wakefulness. I blinked my eyes repeatedly restoring my vision to find them sitting quite separate, humming along to a folk song with a beating drum and the nasally voice of a singer glorifying God.

Upon parking at a turnout next to a tin-roof chai hut, Haider held up his hand in greeting at Shabaz through the foggy van window. Shabaz was just as I imagined. He could have been cut out of the Global article with his crisp *shalwar kameez* as white as the snowy mountains behind him, the contrasting black and white of his light skin framed by the darkest black beard and welcoming onyx eyes that creased when he smiled. Annie and I stepped out of the van into the icy cold. My lungs filled with crisp air that sent a ripple up my spine, satisfying kinks in my back with audible cracks. Annie suggested we both needed a yoga session back at the hotel on our room's tiny balcony.

Haider leaned in for a handshake and Shabaz sandwiched his hands. "How are you, brother Chally?"

"I'm well, Shabaz, but call me Haider." Annie and I were politely greeted by him with a soft *salaam* and his hand to his heart. We reciprocated with *Walaikum salaam* and he bowed gently, causing the swag of his turban's fabric across his shoulder to sway in unison. He tucked his hands into the pockets of his bomber jacket, making the sides of his *kameez* flair out at the hips.

"I hope my broken English will be fine, if not, my Urdu is much better. Neither as fluent as my Pashto."

"Well, brother, between the three languages, we should be able to communicate just fine," Haider spoke.

I added, "Your English is perfect and far better than my Urdu." He accepted the compliment with a generous smile.

He led us to his Jeep, which looked nothing like his neat appearance. Rust corroded the body of the vehicle above the wheels and encircled bullet holes. Shabaz noticed me examining them and confirmed, "They are not bullet holes from any crimes. They are from hunting." Haider elaborated that they were battle wounds from the sportsmen that hunted the Pakistani wild goats.

Annie shyly corrected, "I believe the animal is called the markhor."

"That is right. It is the animal of the Pakistan," Shabaz said proudly.

Haider and Shabaz traded facts about hunting and cars and touched on whether Haider enjoyed the hunting expedition the last time he was here. Haider corrected each time Shabaz called him Chally, insisting he be called Haider. Annie fought to keep herself from bouncing about the Jeep on our rocky climb to the village. I held onto a grab handle that was sadly missing from Annie's side. She'd already bumped the side of her cheek against a metal bar next to the window before I gave her my arm to brace her.

Shabaz warned rockslides from the melting snow could cause delays while he drove up the slim mountain path. Icy gravel crushed underneath the Jeep's tires with each turn of the wheel. Annie pointed to patches of snow crusted on boulders and commented on the heavy snow that hung on the branches of trees. The earthy colors of the landscape broken up by the deep green of trees trying to breathe from beneath the melting snow, was a resplendent sight. I'd seen it at Big Bear Mountain and the Angeles Forest back home on those rare heavy snowfall days in Southern California but it was more contemplative here, more still somehow. For Annie, this was only her second visit to the Quetta mountains and the last time she was here, the snow had thawed.

The path became smoother and Shabaz honked at men wrapped in thick shawls making their way up the path on foot. A goat darted across the road and a little girl ran after it. The appearance of people meant we were getting closer to the Balandi village. Shabaz looked back in lieu of the missing rearview mirror to speak to me.

"Mai and the other women are very much looking forward to meeting with you. Mai wanted to make a big breakfast for you but I said to them to show you the jewelry making and not waste time but they will be most happy if you join them at least for chai later."

"Thank you for considering our time constraints and I'm sure we can join them for a little something," I responded, and Haider gave me a nod validating my courteous answer.

Annie sharply exhaled when we parked and whispered to Haider that she'd hit her head pretty hard against something in the Jeep. He immediately bit his lip and probably regretted not checking her seat belt—a seat belt that wasn't there. Shabaz called me over to two little girls wearing embroidered *shalwar kameezes* under tightly zipped-up jackets. "These are my daughters, Mahgul and Marium." They both giggled *salaams*, clinging to their father. The sun peeked through slowly parting clouds, projecting its light on the smooth marble of the key chain on my bag and bounced off the mirrorwork in their *kameezes*. Shabaz waited for me to say something about his girls. I avoided the usual 'they're beautiful' or 'cute.' Instead, I spoke slowly in Urdu, taking a chance that the girls might understand a few words, "*Mashallah*. It must be nice to have a pair of girls. I'm sure they love you very much." He accepted my version of a compliment with his courteous bow.

His girls scurried away and we walked on together through a dirt path uphill that was the main artery of his tiny village. Annie and Haider's footsteps were close behind. On either side of us were square homes made of some kind of sandstone and some of cement. The sound of a crying baby, the giggles of children, clatter of pots and pans and the snack man's call was softer in the quiet village. The same sounds in Karachi would be magnified, competing over city noise.

I spotted a tall and weathered sandstone building, almost neolithic with exposed mud bricks nearest the ground and wood beams still holding what could have been a centuries old roof. It beamed a warm yellow light; so different from the rest of the homes in color and stature, almost matching the sand-colored skin of the back of my hand. I was distracted from my awe of it by the creaking echo of a snack man's cart making his way up a steep hill with a pile of berries and a mound of root vegetables, and nuts.

When we reached a large opening between the modest homes, Shabaz led us to a tiny house. We were greeted by Mai, her slumped body adorned in a faded orange traditional Balochi *shalwar kameez*, the way I imagined the sunset here to be. When she smiled at me, we exchanged *salaams*. Deep-set wrinkles poured from her heavy eyelids like fireworks.

It took the three of us time to take our boots off before entering her home. Shabaz easily slid his loafers off. Seeing him standing idle, I pulled out the Nisa booklets from my bag and handed them to him to look over. Mai took me by the hand and showed me around her simple home, carpeted with wool rugs, patched with remnants of other rugs. Quiet humming sounds of women's voices came from a back room. A small wood-burning stove with a stool and a simple bed made of wood and intertwining ropes sat nearby. Next to it was a prayer rug with the corner folded like a page of a book.

All of us but Annie had to duck through the small doorway to get into a closet-size room with five women sitting in a circle. A few of them opened tiny metal loops with rusted pliers and others sewed beads onto strings. Each on a different task, each wearing scarves of similar colors, draping their heads. Shabaz asked Mai something in Pashto and one of the women looked up and took a seat on a rug next to Mai. Mai studied my face before she spoke to me. The woman next to her translated what Mai lacked in her Urdu.

"I'm Mai and these women will make your . . ." She spoke in pieces of the Urdu she knew, each word and the sentence structure correct except she stopped short searching for the word for jewelry.

I inserted "*zayvur.*"

Mai smiled a gummy grin and shook her head, "No, I'm Mai and these women will make your . . . Nisa." This woman who used juniper trees and dung to fuel a fire to cook her meals understood that I was not seeking to make jewelry but to start a brand and business that would do more than sparkle against skin.

A chill shot through the front door pressing Mai's scarf against her head and my hair against my back. I asked the translator what her name was and she responded with the plump lips that sat on her tiny rosy face, "Raushan Shams."

"My dadi's name was Shams-un-Nisa." The woman of the sun. It felt like a sign, the way coincidences do when you want them to.

I spoke to Shabaz and Raushan Shams but looked at Mai. "I want to spend the bulk of the day with the women and have them make the sample coin pendant that you said they could. I also want to see where the metals for the jewelry are forged."

"Not a problem. The iron worker is expecting us now." Haider and Annie made their way to the door to get their shoes on. As I began to leave, Mai placed both of her warm hands on mine and pulled me back down.

Looking at me she spoke fluidly in Pashto this time, while Raushan Shams translated, "I've seen the pictures of the kind of jewelry you want. It is not difficult for us to make. We've made jewelry 100 times more complex. We want to make money to care for our families and better our community but we will not work with anyone for any amount of money without knowing who they are and if they're committed. You must make time today to talk with me."

I set my bag down again and held her nearly crippled fingers in my hands and rubbed her paper-thin skin the way I did Dadi Jaan's when I said goodbye to her the last time I saw her. "I feel the same way and would be happy to speak to you over a very simple dinner if it wouldn't be too much trouble."

She clapped her hands in excitement just the way Dadi Jaan had at my request for her famous *aloo parathas*. Mai seemed to be scolding Shabaz when she ushered us out of the door so she could start preparations for dinner, which I assumed would not be as simple as I had requested. Shabaz later explained that I got him in trouble by accepting a dinner invite that he had already declined on our behalf. Once Annie had her boots on, she did a funny-looking jig, excited to be invited to an authentic Balochistani dinner. Haider's dimple appeared on his usually stoic face at her delight.

Two Balandi women from Mai's house followed behind us, one slightly waddled when she walked making the other spry woman slow her pace. The blacksmith's shop was covered with a tin roof and had skinny metal poles for support. In the center was a long metal table and to its side a cement oven resembling a tandoor for pottery. Metal pots clanked together from a steady wind that had nothing to stop it in the open space away from the snuggling homes. Shabaz introduced us to a man wearing a wool *pakol* low on his head and a *shalwar kameez* dotted with tiny burn marks from the embers that were already popping out of the oven.

After a short *salaam* to us, he returned to poking the fire with a long metal stick which he pinched with an oily rag to keep from burning his fingers. The two women that had followed us were placing tiny tools on one end of the long table, keeping to themselves, except for a lingering look exchanged between the waddling woman and the blacksmith. I watched him tinkering with the oven for a bit but grew bored. No sooner, one of the table's legs buckled, reigniting my interest. Haider and Shabaz rushed to help while the blacksmith tried to prop the table back up with a broken stool. We sat ourselves down on a cluster of small boulders nearby and watched until Haider walked over to us.

"I don't know, Haider. Do you think they can produce consistent work?"

Haider huffed at my concern. "This is a poor village, Hena. The man doesn't have the resources he needs. Tools, lack of space. A minimal amount of money and direction could fix that. This is what you wanted to do, remember? Help people like him help you." I didn't like his annoyed tone but accepted his answer.

The glowing red of fire began to roar in the oven. It beckoned our chilled faces and hands closer for thawing. A glowing cup was pulled out with tongs. The blacksmith poured liquified pewter from it into the molds that the women placed near him. They covered their faces with their shawls to protect from the scattering embers and watched from a safe distance. Shabaz pointed to the blackened molds. "They have been passed down for centuries. Everything is touched by the past in some way. The scraps of the metals, the brass, nickel, pewter, and silver are remelted and reused. Also, when a family is needing money, they will sell Mai some of the jewelry that has been in their families for a hundred years sometimes, it is melted down and made new again. The materials keep living even after the people die."

The way Dadi Jaan's *tikka* and *jhumar* and the earrings she'd given me had survived her, I thought. Though, I could never melt them down. They were a part of her and now me.

The spry woman held up a small black mold for me to see, suggesting it would shape the sample pendant I emailed Shabaz sketches of. The first piece of jewelry for Nisa was being forged right in front of me in a country thousands of miles from my home. In this reclusive Balochi village deep in the bewitching mountains, it would be created by humble, skilled artisan hands practicing age-old techniques to produce a bauble that would forever be the priceless pioneering nugget in my collection.

Annie squeezed my shoulder in anticipation as the metal cooled quickly from the chilly air. The blacksmith started on a different project using a soldering machine that shot bluish sparks around our feet, causing us to move back. When the pendant had cooled enough to be handled, but was still malleable, the waddling woman pierced a tiny hole through it with a fine-tip tool. It was handed to the spry one who free-handed a design onto it. She brought the tiny pendant close to her face, smoothed out the edges with a pumice-like rock, and dipped a rag into a container that dripped with a thick black liquid. The liquid would stain the dainty design and make it prominent against its silver background.

They started a similar process with other pieces, unfamiliar to me. I took dozens of pictures of the women working while waiting anxiously to see the final sample piece up close. Annie and Haider both shied away from the camera, allowing me to capture the scene from another epoch altogether without their western attire tainting it.

The blacksmith gestured for the waddling woman to fetch him the pink sack she'd carried with her. Shabaz and the spry one examined something obstructed from my view by a stack of metal pots. A crooked smile warmed the blacksmith's face upon opening the sack. Steam floated out of what appeared to be a bread, prepared by the waddling woman, who stood close to him and rested her hand on her back countering the weight of a now obvious pregnant belly.

Shabaz stood posing one hand on his hip and the other stuck into the side of his turban to satisfy an itch, not taking his eyes off a page in the Nisa booklet. His eyes darted between it and the email version of the same image, which he had printed out.

"Come and see!" His voice echoed around us. The spry woman held out her hand for mine and placed the tiny pendant into it.

The cold object in the center of my warm palm made it feel heavier than it was. It was a rustic coin shape, the way I wanted. I was sure the women would try to smooth it into their interpretation of a machine-made piece. Natural, aged, and the name Nisa etched into it in Urdu called for me to feel its texture. I turned it around and examined it close up. It was identical, not to my sketch in the booklet, but to the image in my mind that couldn't be rendered onto paper.

Haider broke the silence. "What do you think?"

I closed my palm around it to somehow protect its purity from everyone. From under the cover of a tattered rag, another two pendants were displayed for me to examine. Pieces that were mere sketches a few days ago in an email to Shabaz with a note: *Just so you can show the women the style I'm going for.* One was a nickel-size pendant with a tiny mirror held in its center—a popular element in traditional Sindhi and Balochi hats and vests I'd seen hundreds of times. But this one was neatly embedded with prongs, not glued like I'd seen in Karachi. The other, a rough piece of Pakistani jade in a long bar pendant. Annie gasped at the surprise pieces and noticed the trembling of my hands.

Thirteen

Back in the warmth of Mai's house, I tried to process the experience of having three pieces of Nisa come to life. In the modern world, getting an actual product made took months, costly mistakes, second runs, and thousands of dollars. I called my focus to center stage, plopped down on Mai's steps, and spoke in detail with Raushan Shams, Shabaz, and a busy Mai more concerned with burning the onions for the *Dum Pukht* than with the talk she'd said she wanted to have with me.

Flipping through pages of the Nisa booklet to the questions, I jotted down answers about costs, time spent on each piece, and tools used/needed. I also inquired about the women's obvious space constraint, working in Mai's back room, and if there were other options for work spaces anywhere else in the village. When Shabaz pulled away to help settle an argument with two men in the street wielding pieces of papers at each other like weapons, Haider and Annie sat close by, helping me communicate better with Raushan in Urdu.

A heavy lid slammed onto a pot and Mai asked me to come in with Raushan. The aroma of a fragrant broth and basmati rice filled her tiny home.

"How did you like the pendants?" she asked.

"They're exactly as I imagined. I know you're used to making more intricate jewelry."

"Sometimes small and simple pieces can be harder to make because they make us change the way we use our hands but I told them to make the pendants exactly as your sketches. These women are artisans, their mothers were artisans, their daughters will *inshallah* be artisans so long as people still see the value in our work."

Mai was transparent about how much she expected to be paid for each piece and how she would distribute the money to the five women, the blacksmith, and Shabaz. When I did the conversion from rupees to dollars on my phone, I showed it to Haider to confirm the cost of each piece.

"This is nothing, how can she work for so little?"

"You still have to factor in shipping fees and import fees and any business licenses you'll need here and remember . . ."

"It's doable." I whispered to him.

Turning to a page in my booklet, he snaked his finger to the part mentioning 'safe work environment' and 'fair pay' under the heading 'Ethical Practices.'

"Mai, I don't just want to have my jewelry made here. I want the women making it to give me consistent work by being in a proper work space, being safe, supporting themselves, and preserving your tradition." Before Raushan Shams could finish translating, Mai raised her hands to the sky and made a long *dua* praising God and finished with giving me a kiss on the forehead.

"My joints are stiff; I'm going to go stretch outside." Annie smoothed her jacket

Raushan Shams's cheeks glowed pinker after Mai whispered to her. "Mai, wants to know why you aren't married." I could have asked how she knew I wasn't but I'd still have to answer the inevitable question.

"I'm not looking to get married yet. I want to start Nisa first."

Raushan raised an eyebrow, asking her own question. "Aren't your parents unhappy about that?"

"They support my decision . . . but aren't exactly happy about it either."

Mai tapped Raushan on her wrist to stop that line of questioning. When Mai was called by the women working in the back, Haider asked me to join him for a walk. Annie was chatting with Shabaz, admiring the embroidery on his younger daughter's *kameez*, and waved us off when we asked her to come.

"It feels like it's been days since we've spoken but I guess it's just been a busy day," Haider observed.

"It's been overwhelming but in a good way. Still can't believe the pendants came out so well. My head is still spinning."

"I have to admit, I didn't think things would go this well. I hope you seal this deal before we leave tomorrow."

"Like give them the green light, a deposit or something?"

"Maybe more than a deposit. What else do you need them to prove?"

"I still have to get the business and importing licenses. There's still a lot to consider."

"None of that is too difficult. Like you said, it's doable. I can help you get all of that in the works at least before you fly home next week. I could get my Uncle Shafique to help. He helped facilitate the Khewara Mine salt import to the US. I think you guys call it Himalayan pink salt."

"Wow, that's a huge business. I love seeing the *made in Pakistan* label on it versus the vague *from the Himalayas* it used to have."

"I can take you to the bank in Quetta City tomorrow, if you want. You could have a definite start to Nisa right away."

Grains of sand gritted against the soles of our shoes on the steps of the vacant neolithic building where the snow had melted. Through the glassless windows, dust particles floated into a large open space, echoing our footsteps. Haider stretched both arms out making a T-shape as if measuring the area with his body.

"This can be your factory." I admired the contours of his face in the stream of sunlight that came into the sandcastle-like structure. Unfussy in his appearance and grounded in his mind, he was a monolith himself. "There's enough room in the back for the blacksmith too." He pointed to a doorway that led to a newer cemented area outside. I walked through the beams of light and did a twirl, feeling the air resist me.

"It needs plumbing work but it's a huge step up from working in Mai's house."

"Look at these walls, they feel like a mountainside. I can envision the women working in this space but what . . ."

"If, right?"

"Yes, if. I mean I can't just buy a building if that's what you're suggesting. I don't even know what it costs, I haven't spoken to my dad about what I'm doing here or that I'm even here. I can't do everything in one trip."

Small dust clouds kicked up at his feet when he began pacing. "It *is* that easy. You're losing that focus you say you admire so much. Do you realize you've walked into your real-life business idea here? It's like you're afraid to commit. You're clearly afraid."

"I am afraid," I snapped and he stepped back. "What's wrong with being afraid? There's a lot at stake here, Haider. There's the money and making a promise to these women. What if I'm not able to follow through? I don't want to let these poor people down. I need to plan this out first. Tell me, you understand."

"No, I don't understand. I don't understand nonsense. You, yourself don't understand what you're saying either!" He roared the way he did at Annie except this time it echoed and came at me multiple times.

"You said you weren't Musa. Well, I'm not you, Haider. I wasn't taught to make and trust my decisions. This is what it's like to be a woman and not just here but everywhere."

"You have everything at your disposal to make this work. You are making excuses." His words pecked at me.

"This is my decision and I have to make it when it feels right to me."

"I knew this would happen. You'd toy with these people and waste my time too. I'm going back to the hotel." With that he stormed out, leaving a cloud of dust swirling where he stood.

Annie scurried into the building moments after, making me think she was in earshot of us the whole time, "What happened? Don't let him push you into anything. It's a big decision. You should think about it."

"Annie, I really need to be alone right now."

"Are you sure? Ok, sorry, I understand. Shabaz and his wife are waiting to show me their embroidered shawls. I'll be with them. Ok?" Kicking away slushy snow on her way out, she added, "And, Hena, don't worry about Haider."

I sat on the floor where a square of dirt was missing and hung my trembling hands over my knees. It wasn't the cold from the dulling daylight or the lack of sleep. It was the adrenaline from the truth in hearing Haider's hot words. *You're making excuses.* They echoed inside me, bouncing from place to place without escape. Both Omar and Haider, two people worlds apart, one who'd known me my entire life and the other only a few days, had pointed out the same obvious flaw in me. When Omar brought it to my consciousness, it propelled me to come to Pakistan with the possibility of starting Nisa. Now, I was frozen with fear at the sight of seeing its birth.

Instincts, feelings, reasons, and excuses were all mixing together making things unclear. I wrapped my arms around my knees when a strong gust blew into the vacant building. The warmth of my own body settled me a bit; something heavy to keep my anxious soul from floating away. The weight of my phone in my coat pocket reminded me that I could call any of my loved ones and ask for advice, except one— Dadi Jaan. What would each of them counsel? What would Dadi Jaan advise? Probably, hold me close and tell me no decision I made would be wrong, it would just be. Whenever Dadi Jaan entered my mind, my heart pumped grief and love at the same time and quieted me somehow.

Icy wind moved around me, touching the back of my neck with its cold fingers. It didn't make me shiver, instead it began to travel up my nasal passages to fill my lungs and expand a hungry belly. I finally began to breathe with intent: scent of dried apricots from the snack cart outside, an after-the-rain smell from melting snow, and the faintest fragrance of tea rose perfume rising from my coat that I couldn't smell earlier. Feeling revived, I knew what I wanted to do, not for Mai, the women, Haider, Baba, or Dadi Jaan's memory but for myself. It was time again to cross a threshold, pulling fear along with me by the hand, kicking and screaming.

❖

The aroma of Mai's cooking wafted through the tiny village. Neighborhood children gathered around her house hoping she'd dish some out to them. I spotted Annie's red jacket behind a rusty barrel on the corner of Mai's house. She pressed her hand over her giggling mouth to keep from alerting the children to her hiding place.

"Are you ok?" She nudged me and ducked down deeper.

"I'm ok. Actually, I feel a lot better." I whispered and a seriousness replaced her smile.

"Are you going to do it? You know you don't have to make a decision right now?"

"I know."

Large block-printed bed sheets were placed over Mai's rugs, transforming her home into a dining hall. Two large silver platters of *Dum Pukht* sat on each end, the rice piled high with morsels of lamb sprinkled with almonds and raisins that glistened with *ghee*. In between the platters were mismatched plastic bowls of yogurt, sliced raw onions, and radishes. Mai, the blacksmith, the five women, and a few men, most likely some of their husbands took turns feeding the toddlers who buzzed back and forth between them.

Annie and I were tucked in between Mai and Raushan Shams. When Shabaz, his wife, and their little girls took their seats, Mai's house was packed full.

Shabaz called from the men's end of our aromatic buffet, "Where is Haider, Annie *baji*?"

"He started walking towards the hotel to get better cell reception. He needed to make some calls. Don't worry, he said to start without him. I'm sure he's enjoying the Balandi views." Annie avoided eye contact with him and unnecessarily recentered the bowl of yogurt and onions in front of us. His flaring nostrils turned his otherwise pleasant face into a grimace.

"What did you think of the samples?" Shabaz asked, unloosening his daughter's embrace from around his neck. Mai scolded us for talking about work over food, saying that food spoiled with such talk. Not wanting to invite any bad omens over our feast, we amused ourselves with small talk about the stark differences in weather in various parts of Pakistan. Annie spoke about her grandmother's ties to Balochistan and even the Kalash people further up in the North. I ate the rich meal with a newfound appetite, my fingers greasy with the rice that was coated in lamb fat and *ghee*.

Annie clicked her tongue at me and showed me the proper technique of eating rice with the hands. It required pressing the rice into the plate and simultaneously closing the tips of the fingers to compact it to avoid the trail of rice I was leaving from plate to mouth. I could have perfected it but the heaviness of the meal began to slow me down.

Mai noticed and pressed for me to "*Khwarhal, Khwarhal!*"

Raushan translated, "eat, eat" as urgently as Mai spoke it, though I'd know its meaning even if it was in Morse Code.

"She sounds just like my dadi," I told Annie as Mai placed a piece of lamb on my plate with her fingers, the way Mom used to pick out the leanest pieces of meat from a pot of biryani for me to eat. Mai must have incurred quite an expense feeding us but she hosted us as generously as a Mughal empress, sparing no expense for her honored guests.

The guests had trickled out of the house by the time night fell, the elders wrapped themselves in thick wool shawls and sat on Mai's porch for a fried bread dessert sprinkled with brown sugar. A pink chai, the color of Himalayan pink salt, studded with crushed pistachios, warmed my hands while Annie and I leaned in the doorway watching the neighborhood children make up dances.

Raushan Shams alerted me that the dessert of *mithai* I had her sent for, for Annie's birthday, had arrived. I slipped away with her to the back of the house where she gathered the children to make a small procession. The children fought over who got to hold the two sparklers Shabaz was able to find. I carried the plate of *mithai*, and Raushan and the children, familiar with the universal happy birthday song, began on my cue.

Annie covered her mouth, hiding her teeth but not her surprise. "Happy Birthday Annie. Surprise!"

"You are too much, Hena. Thank you for remembering!"

Annie insisted on serving her new friends first, the children she'd played hide-and-seek with earlier. I asked Mai and Raushan Shams if I could speak to them alone. Mai led us through a curtained doorway to the workroom, away from the noise of the excited children.

"Thank you for everything today. I've decided that I would like to start my business with you. If possible, I'm going to try to secure a better space for you all to work. Maybe, the empty building at the mouth of the village but I'm going to start Nisa here with you."

I reached into my bag and placed rupees roughly the equivalent of $1,000 US dollars, wrapped in scratch paper, into Mai's folded hands. "This means I'm committing to work with you. I'll be going down to Quetta city tomorrow to set some things up and be back with more information before I leave for Karachi." Annie tapped on the window, blew her warm breath on the glass and wrote an H with her finger. I peeked out of the curtain and saw Haider at the front door in a squat untying his laces.

With the money still in her hand, she held my face with her hands to kiss my forehead before reciting a quiet prayer.

"Can we please talk?" Haider asked me.

"Don't take your shoes off, let's talk outside."

Shabaz stopped us while we searched for a quiet place in the neighborhood. "You missed dinner. They said you were walking around?"

"I regret not joining you for dinner. I went for a long walk while the women did their business."

Shabaz stared blankly at Haider, hoping he would add more to his explanation. When Shabaz's daughter came up to him with a piece of *mithai*, he left us to join the others.

"Listen, Hena. You know what I'm going to say. I shouldn't have been angry with you. You have a right to be afraid."

"I appreciate you saying that."

"You gave Mai something . . . was it money?"

"I've decided to take the leap."

The corners of his mouth made a slow rise until he couldn't contain a bursting smile.

"I want to go into town tomorrow and find out what licenses I need and, Haider, I do want to inquire about that vacant building. I realize I may need to stay here longer. I know you have to get back to the shop and Annie back to work and your mom, I'm sure. I'll call my dad and fill him in on everything. He knows people in Quetta who could help me too and, if not, who knows maybe, he may want to fly out himself."

"I could stay here another few days if you still need me that is." He moved in closer, searching for my reaction.

"You know I still need your help but I don't know what to do with your temper with Annie and . . . me too."

"You've got quite a temper too. You had me a little scared earlier." He snorted and changed the subject. "I don't know how much money you've given to Mai and it's not my business anyway but if you want to undertake real estate and licenses, it's going to take quite a bit."

"I have it." Whispering, I clutched my bag.

Annie and I waved bye to Mai and her family from the back of Shabaz's Jeep. Children ran behind us shouting Annie's name as we drove away. Their cheers disappeared once we passed the entrance of the village marked by two rusty barrels.

"You will never be let down working with the Balandi people, I promise you this." Shabaz looked back and spoke loudly, assuring me.

Annie, however, asked in her meek voice, barely audible over the sounds of the rough terrain under the Jeep's wheels, "Are you really going to do it?"

"Yes. I am"

"I wish you'd wait until we got back to Karachi. You have to discuss it with your family."

Haider pressed his head against the headrest to speak to us, "She will, Annie. Hena, I suggest you call your dad after you get all the information in the city tomorrow."

"I agree."

"Hena, you can do all that by making a few phone calls when you get back to Karachi."

Annie seemed to be pleading with me, the whites of her big eyes glowed in the dark of the car.

"Why don't you want me to do this? Did you see something about Mai or the women that makes you cautious?"

Moving back into her seat with only her silhouette visible in the dark, she shook her head *no*. We sat quietly the rest of the way and when we arrived at the hotel, Shabaz told me he'd be in town and could be reached easily if I needed anything. Since cell reception was nonexistent in the village we could only communicate if he was near the hotel or in the city below.

When I thanked him for the help he'd provided, he placed his hand on his heart and praised, "It's all because of the Almighty, I deserve no credit." His submission to God's decree further sweetened my resolve to work with him and the others.

His kind of faith, I'd heard only from the poor in Pakistan. Like the women sitting on the side of the street selling knick knacks to laborers and the neighborhood snack man, the one with the ricketiest cart and worn sandals. When Baba complimented the snack man's mangos or his jujubes, he glorified God. What many non-Muslims considered a limiting belief, Muslims found liberating. If fruit trees yielded smaller fruit one season, the farmer didn't grieve. Instead, he accepted that he played only a small part in the outcome of his crop. Likewise, he wouldn't boast that he mastered his trade by producing the sweetest fruit around. With either outcome, he would surrender to God's higher plan for his life.

THE FATIGUE FROM OUR EVENTFUL day set in the moment we stepped into the hotel lobby. Our feet had to drag our bodies up the stairs. Haider asked Annie to come to his room to give her the birthday present. I rushed into mine to fire off texts to Baba and Chacha, relieving them of any worry they may have had not being able to reach me all day, and I promised to video call them tomorrow.

Eventually, I washed up and got busy looking up business bureaus and import fees. Annie walked in massaging her temples. She sat at the edge of the bed without the new purse I'd expected her to be ecstatic about.

"Thank you from the bottom of my heart for the surprise today. I think you're an amazing person and I love you. I'm sorry that I couldn't help you."

"What are you talking about? You've helped me enormously."

The door handle to our room squeaked and Haider stuck his head in, "Annie, take something for that headache and get some sleep before it gets worse"

"I will." She nipped and stomped her way into the bathroom.

"You should get some sleep too."

He handed me a cup of tea. A spiced minty steam flowed from it, warming my face, "Did you give her the present?"

"I forgot to pack it. I told her about it though. Anyway, I just wanted to tell you that it'll be just you and me tomorrow. Annie's going to stay back. Dealing with the business end of this will bore her."

New ideas inspired by the embroidery of the Balandi women's *kameezes* kept me plugged to my sketch tablet. After I finished the tea, I gave myself permission to sleep. With my tired arm, I pushed my heavy bag and tablet under the bed and concluded tomorrow would be as triumphant as today.

Fourteen

The wind knocking at the balcony door woke me. Though my vision was oddly fuzzy, I could make out that sunshine showed like afternoon light on the floral wallpaper. The bathroom light peeking through the bottom of the door meant I'd have to wait to empty my bladder. I blindly felt around on the nightstand for my phone so I could check the time, but couldn't locate it. Thinking the short charging wire might have pulled it to the floor, I rolled to my side to reach around for it under the bed and came up empty-handed. I crouched beside the bed and pulled my hair out of the way to look underneath the bed but the phone wasn't there either. Neither was my bag.

"Annie," I called out, restraining the panic in my voice just in case I found it somewhere else in the room, but it was gone and so was Annie. The balcony door still knocked, wind whistling through its cracks like a tea kettle as I searched the room for my bag, my tablet, or for Annie's things, her red jacket, anything - and came up with nothing.

I forcefully pulled the room door open causing it to bump the wall and ran across the hall to Haider's room. A cleaning lady hiking up her *shalwar* preparing to sweep the bathroom floor looked at me as if waiting for instruction. When she saw me nearly stumble my way back to my room, she came after me, concerned. Her mouth moved but her words faded in and out of my hearing. With slow, deliberate steps I moved towards the balcony, hoping to see the van safe in its parking spot outside. The doors of the balcony parted gracefully upon a gentle turn of the handles. Wind that knocked softly on the balcony doors earlier shouted icy air against my skin.

Other than the porter chasing a piece of trash and the honeymooning couple taking selfies near their car, the parking lot sat almost vacant. Grasping the cold railing with clammy hands, my knees made a slow descent to the tiled balcony floor. When the cleaning lady shook me, unsticking my sweaty forehead from the railing I leaned against, the thumping sound of my heartbeat faded.

She got me into the armchair but I don't remember how or when. The manager of the hotel and a blurry figure of a short man and the tearing sound of a blood pressure monitor's Velcro cuff being pulled apart hung over me. Eventually, I was able to form the sentence that alerted them that my two friends had taken off with a large sum of my money.

Within half an hour, two policemen in uniform and a lanky police investigator in civilian clothes, with eyeglasses that rested on his forehead, gathered in the room. "I'm Investigator Idrees Khan and what is your name?"

"Hena Shah."

"And do you have any identification?"

"No. They took everything . . . tablet, my copy of the Nisa booklet, money, and my passport. I just have that duffle bag of my clothes and this coat."

I held the sleeve of my tweed coat, which hung on the armchair, close to my chest for comfort.

"You said money. Please elaborate." His primary concern was money, but Haider and Annie had taken the breath from my lungs. They'd taken with it a lifelong collection of ideas in my sketch tablet and with my passport, my way home.

Peeking through the armoire and lifting the blanket with the back of his pen, he asked what I was doing with such a large amount of money, who Annie and Haider were, but paused when I mentioned Shabaz's name. Well acquainted with Shabaz and the Balandi village, the hotel manager immediately called Shabaz to come in. The concierge was called up and vouched for Annie and Haider being guests at the hotel and also confirmed they left in a rush at dawn, ignoring him when he asked if they were checking out early.

Noticing the sunlight weaken and move its pattern on the wallpaper to the ceiling, I asked a policeman for the time. "It is 4:34, miss."

"It's evening? I just woke up. I don't understand!"

"Is this your tea?" Investigator Khan wrinkled his forehead, making his eyeglasses land on the bridge of his nose and sniffed the cup.

"I'm not certain but you may have been given a strong sleeping aid, if not something more dangerous."

The doctor chimed in, looking closely at my eyes, "Earlier your vision and hearing were impaired too. It is possible."

Shabaz was told to meet the detective in the lobby for questioning. By the time they both came up to the room, the manager closed the balcony doors and offered me a blanket to keep warm. Upon seeing Shabaz's solemn face, I wanted to cry out to him but questioned his involvement with Annie and Haider.

"Were you a part of this, Shabaz? How long have you known Haider?" I wanted the same answers the detective must have asked him privately but I wanted to hear it for myself.

"Allah is my witness, I had nothing to do with this and I will tell you everything honestly."

He began with the same information we'd exchanged via email about how he met Haider at an expo in Karachi. He was then hired to take Haider and his musician friends on a game-hunting expedition but was unable to take the job upon their arrival, giving the task to his friend, Hakeem. He explained that he was instead at the Quetta Civil Hospital collecting his father's body to perform his final rites before the burial. Investigator Khan himself had attended the funeral.

He patted Shabaz's back and asked him not to leave the area on any travel until he was cleared, to which he replied "Where would I go? I live here."

Before he left, he knelt down beside me. "I can ask Mai to give you your deposit money back." To which I weakly replied, "no".

"Miss Hena, we will do our best to find them but in the meantime, you should get in touch with your consular office and notify them of the theft of your passport if you want to be able to return to the US anytime soon," he warned.

The cleaning lady ushered me to the bathroom for a shower. Without my phone and no numbers or addresses committed to memory, I was useless to the police in contacting anyone. Investigator Khan would do a search to find Chacha's number and convey the details of the crime to him and the Karachi police, relieving me of the painful chore in a frazzled condition.

When I turned the shower on, the noise of the policemen's boots and conversations with the hotel staff faded. The thought of the calls that would be made to Chacha and then Baba by the police filled me with horrifying shame. It knotted all the passages from my heart to my brain, the hollowness of my stomach felt as if I hadn't eaten for days. Every part of me wanted to be washed down the dark drain and never be found again, but I knew I'd have to face it all.

A knock at the door by the cleaning lady telling me that my family was on the phone brought the inevitable to me without any time for preparation. The room had been cleared so I could change and speak to Chacha in private. I cried the instant I heard his hello. Chacha's words gushed, as he started with, "What's done is done. I tried booking myself a flight to escort you back but your baba very angrily insisted I stay put. He's sent Surghum to get you by car; said he knew what was best."

Baba instinctively knew I wouldn't be able to keep myself together if Chacha started interrogating me on the flight home and that the only flight I would want to take now would be home to him. Surghum would bring me back safely and follow Baba's instructions to the letter.

Broken by sobs, I asked Chacha, "What was Baba's reaction to this?"

"He's worried about you. He wants you to come home safely. Just stay put."

How the night set and the next day rose for me in that room I could not explain. A numbness had begun to seep into my broken soul. I lay in the same tight position all night for fear that allowing my body to move would push my delicate psyche over the edge to free fall into oblivion.

Surghum greeted me in the same way he'd always done. A quick *"Salaam,* Hena bibi," followed by a rush to transport me to wherever I needed to be. In this case, the long journey back to the metropolis of Karachi and eventually back home to Baba. Surghum's eyes bugged out at the sight of the fine dust and mud splatters that had streaked the car. After closing the car door behind me, he pulled his sleeve cuff over his hands to wipe my window clean but stopped himself, realizing it would take more than that to fix the mess.

I sat snuggled against the car door, my head pressed to the side of the window taking the occasional thump as we passed over bumps on the highway. When Surghum couldn't avoid making wide U-turns at gas stations along the way, I slid across the seat and huddled back into the same corner of the car where it felt safe.

Surghum kept his interaction with me minimal other than asking me if I needed anything. I asked for water and nothing else. He brought me a water bottle and a bag of chips. When we were halfway home, I opened the bag. At the sound, Surghum's exhausted eyes turned up into a satisfied smile. Instantly, nausea set in from the scent but I forced two crispy pieces down my throat.

Dirt devils swirled in the distance and calmed into nothing. Magically the scenery began changing from snowy passes to the arid tundra of the Balochistan desert. We passed the same roadside restaurant where Haider had stormed out of the car. I replayed every word the two of them had ever spoken to me, every side glance I caught them give each other, every touch he and I shared, Annie's last utterance to me, "I'm sorry that I couldn't help you," and Haider's subtle suggestions about money and blatant pushiness. I didn't care that it all made sense now. I felt nothing where vehement emotions should have been.

Driving into the city, the night call to prayer echoed from every mosque. An hour later, we entered Mausumbe Road. A boy leisurely crossed in front of our car attempting to retrieve a wicket on the street, possibly from an earlier game of cricket. Surghum grunted at him to move along and I stared at the boy's smug face.

"Stop!" I shouted, breaking the seal of my lips. I slid across the seat and left the car, leaving the door ajar. Momentum urged me on to press hard against the bell at the gate of Haider's house. I knew he wouldn't magically answer. He was probably in another city, but I pressed the bell again and again for something to happen, for someone to answer me.

A man in an untucked dress shirt I assumed to be a tenant at the house appeared at the gate, he adjusted his glasses to get a closer look at me in the dark.

"*As-salaam alaikum?*"

"I need to see Haider's mom." I said. He wrinkled his face in confusion.

"Where are Haider and Annie? Where is their mother?"

"You are Sheena Auntie's niece, right?"

Gasping for air I asked for Haider again.

"Sorry, I don't understand. I am Haider." I gripped the side of the gate to prevent myself from falling. Another set of footsteps approached.

"No, you're not him. Ok, then I need to see his mother."

The throaty voice of an older woman called, "Haider, who is it?" The man asked her to come to the door and introduced her as his mother, Tabassum Begum.

She struggled to stand and leaned on her son for support. Her plump body filled a crisp yellow *shalwar kameez*. "Ami, this is Sheena Auntie's niece." She tilted her head. "Your dadi was a beloved friend and she spoke about you every time I visited with her. *Mashallah*, how grown you are now."

My breathing slowed for a moment at the mention of Dadi Jaan.

"Your name is Haider? Is there another Haider that lives here? A girl named Annie?"

"Annie, yes, but first, I'm Haider Ghelani and there is no other Haider that lives here. Annie and her husband, Ali, used to rent out our second story but they moved out only two days ago."

"Her husband?" My insides shrieked.

When my body swayed and I struggled to stand, Surghum noticed and interjected, "Hena bibi, maybe you should get home and rest."

"Surghum, who is this guy?" I asked in hurried words, looking for confirmation for what I was being told. He offered a *salaam* to the man and his mother, stating their names as Haider Saab and Tabassum Begum.

"I don't believe it," I snapped and pushed my way through them, running into their house. On the bottom floor, a Pakistani soap played with weepy music in the background, in the bedroom a laptop lay open to a YouTube video on how to fix a leaky tap. Not a single dirty dish in the kitchen sink and tea about to boil over on the stove. I swung myself around an ironing cove near the back door that led up a stairway to the second floor where Haider and Annie had apparently lived. The man and his mother's steps followed me into the house and Surghum rushed in calling after me.

The second floor was as empty as the vacant building in Balandi. Balled up pieces of newspaper sat at the feet of a plastic chair facing an open window that gave full view of my rooftop yoga. I'd been preyed on by a calculating couple. A river of tears should have streamed out of me if I could have mustered the strength to form them.

"Hena bibi, please. This is not appropriate. Let's go home. You can let the police handle it."

"Police?" the old woman questioned.

Surghum held up his palm to her, insisting, "Please, we will talk to you about it later."

In the driveway of our house, Shenachi wrapped her arm around my waist and practically carried me to my room. A fruit cup and a small plate of fluffy turmeric rice with a jug of water sat on a tray on a folding table—the same as Dadi Jaan had had once, she grew too sick and weak to join the rest of the family at the dinner table. No one said a word.

Fifteen

In the morning I gave my statement to the Karachi Police, another investigator, and to a Mr. Ejaz with the Counter Terrorism Department whose presence felt unnecessary. A vague explanation of protocols that had to be followed were given about why he was there. When a police report had to be submitted with my request for an emergency passport, the American Consulate sent Mr. Ejaz in to do their own investigation before approving the passport. The close proximity of the crime to the Afghanistan and Iran borders meant they weren't going to call the stolen passport a typical theft.

Over countless cups of chai, which was the only thing I could stomach, I robotically retold the story of meeting Annie and Haider and our excursion to the Balandi village. Shenachi was given the task of asking the question the police felt was inappropriate to ask me themselves: had I been sexually assaulted in any way? Names of people I had come in contact with in Karachi were of interest to them and the only people I could name were Skinner and Musa.

Later, in a detailed report I would read that Skinner was the sole owner of the music store, where Haider was simply an employee on and off for the past year. Annie did however work at the tutoring center with three students who all knew her by a different name. Just like Haider's music students, Skinner and even Shabaz knew him by his nickname, Chally—a name fitting of Haider's sneaky character derived from the story of *Ali Baba and the Forty Thieves*. So telling and yet I missed it. Each revelation pained me like a splitting wound.

A few accusing questions implying I was in cahoots with Haider and Annie were raised that fell flat, since it was my money, they'd taken off with. Still, the investigation continued to tiptoe around my motives for traveling with Annie and Haider. Was it my plan to run away from my family to start a new life? Chacha stepped in to defend me, his eyes glued to me, searching for affirmation as he spoke, "She's an independent adult woman who could excommunicate from family if she wanted to without all this pretense."

Despite Shenachi's request to keep the matter private, the Ghelani family was being questioned across the street with no leads to Annie and Haider or their real identities. When I grew weak with exhaustion with their lengthy questioning and sequencing of events that poked at fresher wounds, I wanted to tell them that the case was simple. It was two criminals, one who befriended me, one who bed me, both of whom saw the apparent cracks in me and slid through to take advantage.

Bushra Auntie rang twice wanting to know what the police cars were doing on the street. The actual Haider Ghelani came by to give the FBI director the numbers he'd found of two references Annie had provided prior to renting his space. One was a disconnected number and the other, Annie's uncle from Sialkot, who told the police he too was looking for Annie and her husband, who'd swindled him out of his modest savings. He insisted his naïve niece's tricky husband went by various different names, none of them Haider, Chally or Ali, which only a few of the neighbors knew him by. He showed some concern for Annie's health issues which he confirmed were a result of a tragic accident. He suggested the investigators look into hospitals and migraine treatment centers in Karachi to see if Annie was being treated there. He explained it was something he'd heard the pair talk about. The last he'd heard from either of them was nearly a year ago before they left Sialkot and vanished.

Even though Haider Ghelani only stayed in the doorway of the living room for a few moments and didn't see me coiled up in the corner of the couch, I saw him. A beam of sunlight across his face illuminated the chocolate brown of his eyes when he pushed the sharp strands of his hair away from his forehead, the way I remembered him doing as a kid and the way the pseudo-Haider never did.

Later that day, I sat alone on the porch with a cup of tepid chai where the sounds of Annie's laughter and Haider's serenade in my head were gone, replaced by the slow chirping of birds returning home for the evening. Chacha brought me a temporary phone to use to speak to Baba. Reluctantly I pressed to call him. Baba answered but I couldn't speak so he started.

"I've spoken to the detective from Quetta and just got off the phone with the Deputy Inspector General in Karachi. Thia Kuli knows him and set the call up for me. Kuli is good for something after all. The inspector said that the investigators are going to do their part to find the perpetrators and I told them that I wasn't concerned with what they had to do. I just don't want them to make you stick around waiting. Anyway, you should be given the all clear to travel in a day or two."

"Baba." I paused and couldn't say more. An apology for being a disaster of a daughter clung to the walls of my throat, never making it out of my mouth.

His voice cracked when he spoke. "Just come home. I've kept everything a secret from your mom. Omar knows and blames himself for encouraging you. He's worried and wants you to come home." I couldn't speak but even if I could, what words would suffice?

I CLOSED THE DAINTY CURTAINS in Dadi Jaan's window after seeing Surghum's reflection, busily loading my suitcase, on the freshly washed car. Little Saadia stood close by monitoring him, moving her hand side to side, giving suggestions on how to best fit it in the trunk. Surghum shooed her away to tell me it was time to head out. I opened the door that led to the porch to exit Dadi Jaan's room for the last time. A backdraft of air rushed in swaying the curtains and lifting the edges of the bed skirt off the ground the way it did when I first arrived.

Alone in the room, I spoke to the air that seemed to be guiding me from the conception of this trip.

"Good bye, Dadi Jaan."

Chacha slapped the tears from his cheeks and Shenachi rubbed his back. I gave them long hugs whispering thank-yous and *salaams* to them. Surghum and I started down Mausumbe Road without looking back. Soon he was humming a song; its melody I'd memorized.

"How old are your kids?"

"Twenty two, twenty and thirteen." He gushed about their academic accomplishments and pointed to the sky, thanking Allah for the education he was able to afford them through his job for my family. He was still talking when we arrived at the airport.

"Thank you for making the long trip to Quetta to bring me home."

He straightened his *kameez* and delivered the usual yet poignant line of sweet surrender, "It was all by Allah's will, Hena bibi. That's how we get anywhere."

I suppose that's how I found and lost a friend, heard the heat of music for the first time sung to me by someone destined to break my heart. I met the Balandi women living in their mountaintop village who gave birth to Nisa from the womb of a coal-filled furnace. I'd been lied to and stolen from. On my face, my loved ones saw the lines of shame appear where a smile once sat. The fear of falling and failing tried hard to suffocate me but I'd go on…by God's will, I suppose.

Clouds floated by and vanished outside the plane's window. Daylight turned to starlight but I kept my mind's screen on, foreseeing my life ahead. There would be periods of excruciating sadness and I'd get through by meeting Baba for chai in the tea parlor, holding my nephew's chubby fingers, and planning a baby shower for his little sister who would join him, Omar, and Ayesha. There would be declarations to Mom to desist from hurling her expectations at me and forcefully hugging her to smooth away her sharp edges, no matter how much she resisted. I envisaged reconnecting with Ameer but never marrying him.

I knew I'd return to the Balandi village, this time with Baba, and bypass Karachi altogether, to carry on where I left off with Nisa, allowing the wind to gently swirl around us in the once-vacant building. I could see how hard I'd fallen from an edge and how it hurt more than I ever imagined it could, but I was still breathing.

Glossary

Asalaam alaikum - Muslim greeting meaning peace be upon you

As-salaam - Attribute of God, meaning The source of peace

Baji - Sister

Barfi - A confection made of milk, sugar and cardamom resembling fudge

Beta - Son

Beti - Daughter

Bismillah - Arabic for in the name of Allah

Bun kebab - Pakistani style burger

Chacha - Youngest paternal uncle

Chalees - 40 in Urdu

Chuthth pay - On the rooftop

Dada - Paternal grandfather

Dadi/dadi jaan - Paternal grandmother. Jaan is a term of endearment having various meanings, most commonly used in conjunction with a family member's title.

Dum Pukht - Balochistani rice pilaf made with lamb

Dua - Supplication

Dupatta - Scarf or shawl

Ghee - Clarified butter

Gora - Fair skinned usually used to refer to a white man

Inshallah - Arabic for God willing

Jhumkay - Chandelier earrings

Jins - As in genie or ghost like beings

Khaas - A particular thing

Khewara Mine - Salt caves in Pakistan that produce Himalayan Pink Salt

Lota - A pitcher vessel used for water as a mobile bidet

Maidan - A field; part of a tabla

Masala - Savory mix of spices

Mashallah - A praising of God when witnessing good in a person or event.

Mausumbe - Orange (fruit)

Mithai - A colorful assortment of fudge like confections

Nihari - Gravy like stew made with chunks of beef shank and bone marrow

Nikah - Islamic marriage

Paan - Betel nut leaf, rose jam and betel nut pieces; mouth refresher and snack having properties of a mild narcotic

Paan-daan - A small container with compartments that hold the various ingredients to make paan

Pakol - A wool hat

Pakola - Pakistani soda with a rosy flavor

Paratha - Pan fried flat bread

Rizq - Blessings; often food or money

Roti/s - An unleavened flat bread made with wheat

Salaam alaikum – Short form of Muslim greeting meaning peace be upon you

Salan - Thin gravy like curry and stews

Shahada - Islamic testimony or reaffirmation of faith.

Shalwar kameez/es -Traditional Pakistani clothing consisting of harem style pants (shalwar) and long tunic top (kameez)

Shami Kebab - Burger like patties made with minced meat and lentils

Shavasana - Corpse Posture in yoga; usually practiced at the end of a yoga routine

Siahi - Referring to a part of the tabla (musical instrument)

Tabla/s - Musical instrument with twin hand drums originating from India and Pakistan

Thia - Eldest paternal uncle

Tikka and Jhumar - Usually bridal jewelry worn low on the forehead and one side of head

Ullu kay putthay - Curse word in Urdu meaning son of an owl; an idiot

Unda paratha - Pakistani breakfast of fried eggs and pan fried flat beard.

Walaikum salaam - Muslim greeting reply meaning and upon you be peace.

Zakat - charity obligatory on Muslims; one of the five tenets of Islam

Zayvur – Jewelry

Acknowledgments

Many thanks to the talented and kind people who were instrumental in making this novel possible. I would like to acknowledge Charles Roberts, who, years ago, gave this freelance journalist a by-line. This helped me to see the value in my voice. I am grateful for the legacy of my earliest inspiration and mentor, my maternal grandfather – a journalist and one of the founders of the first newspapers in Pakistan and my paternal grandmother – matriarch and fierce storyteller. I am incredibly thankful to my skilled and supportive editor Brooke Goode, who gave astute comments and magically understood Urdu words without an initial glossary. Thank you to Saaleh Patel, my British-Pakistani proofreader, for combing through the multilingual usage in this book. Thank you to Galag Studio and Fatima Khan for dodging Karachi traffic to get the best shots for a cinematic book vibe trailer. Thank you to Fahad and Asad for being my liaisons in Karachi. Also, gratitude to the Ali family in Karachi for the use of their quiet home during the research part of this novel. I am indebted to my parents for their lifelong sacrifices that created opportunities for me to do what I love. A big thank you to my publicist, Erin Cernuda for her advice: "lean into it." It was more empowering than she knew. For the generous gift of time, space, and for believing in me, I thank Shaan Johri. He has always been an eager audience to this storyteller. Finally, thanks and praise be to Allah, the writer of all life.

www.ingramcontent.com/pod-product-compliance
Lightning Source LLC
Chambersburg PA
CBHW031529310726
48971CB00008B/2408